The Bastard Dragon
The Covert Dragons Book 1

By

Viola Grace

Trin has been raised with the knowledge that her parentage was unknown and she was human. Those two items were the cornerstone of her existence.

An altercation at a baby shower leads to her discovering another side to herself. That side was big, crystalline, and caused the other dragons in her vicinity to bow their heads. Defending her friend had led her into this new shape, and now, she was stuck with it.

Taken to the central hub of the dragon council, she trades her cooperation for knowledge and freedoms. She had been an independent woman a lot longer than she had been a dragon, and she wasn't going to lose her lifestyle just because she could suddenly breathe blasts of pure energy.

Along the way, she learns about where she came from, and it gives her an outline for the life she wants, with the dragon of her choosing.

Chapter One

$\mathcal{I}$rin grinned at the barista who had just arrived to begin his shift. "Running a little late, Tobias?"

Tobias blushed slightly and hung up his coat. He rolled up his cuffs and tied on his apron. "The rain slowed the traffic."

She pulled the handle of the steamer and leaned back as the cloud of vapour warmed the milk to just shy of scalding. "Uh, huh. The weather seems to kick in every time you have an evening shift."

"It is just luck." He winked.

"For someone with four rabbit's feet,

you are surprisingly unlucky." She poured the waiting espresso shots into the cup and walked it around to the customer's table.

"Here you go."

The regular smiled. "Thank you, Trin. Are you escaping?"

"Trin! The machine is stuck!"

Trin closed her eyes for a moment, inhaled and exhaled. "I am getting away as soon as the equipment is functioning."

The woman chuckled, sipped at her coffee, and lifted her book. Trin walked back to the counter, and she assessed the situation. Tobias was filling the orders for regular coffee, but the specialty orders had to wait.

Humming softly, she went to the back office and got her toolkit. The an-

and put her tools away, adding a new washer to her shopping list. Working with a fifty-year-old machine made it a draw for the patrons, but it took a lot of maintenance to keep the gears, wheels, and pistons working all day long.

When the equipment was tucked away, she scrubbed her hands and took her apron off. Her open skirt was mildly wrinkled, but that was part of her charm. She was always wrinkled or mussed or scruffy. It was part of the fun of being human in a city filled with shapeshifters.

She grabbed her jacket and folded it over her arm. Slinging her small purse strap around her wrist, she checked the shop one more time, and then, she left for the day.

The bell rang as she exited, and she

crossed the small paved walkway that ran between Harbinger Coffee and Harbinger Tea. With the success of the coffee shop, Brenner had asked if they could expand to tea, and she had not seen any reason not to. Now, each coffee shop that they owned had a teashop across the walkway. It satisfied both of their target demographics and let everyone get home at a reasonable time in the evening.

When the bell rang as she opened the door, she heard laughter from inside. There were two small groups of women murmuring and giggling. It was a sound that Trin loved to hear.

She walked toward a counter, and a tea tier was placed in front of her. "Thanks, Niida."

Niida chuckled. "You are late. Tobias

again?"

"Yes. I am going to have to put my foot down. Eventually."

"Trin, you are too easygoing."

She shrugged. "I am. It doesn't matter to me. I could do the whole day there."

Niida's eyes widened. "Don't you dare. Brenner is really competitive, and the next thing I know, I would be missing a husband."

Trin snorted. "Bren is yours, he wouldn't spend any time more than necessary out of your company."

"You have a seat, I will bring your tea." Niida smiled.

Trin took her tray with its treats, and she walked to one of the small empty tables. The seat cushion invited her to lean back, so she did.

Looking around the neat shop, she saw the touches that Brenner had asked her to add. An antique kettle with a hand-cranked gearing system to ignite the flame that boiled the water. It was something that could have taken up less than a square foot, but he had asked her to make a long chain of twisting gears and rotating links to finally spark the ignitor. It was a new piece designed to look old, and it didn't require much maintenance. It was kind of cool.

Niida swished around the counter, her cascade of brilliant burgundy hair was lying in a thick braid over one shoulder. Brenner had gotten very lucky with this vixen. His fox had never been so happy as he was the day they said their vows. When Trin visited their home, they were often frolicking in their beast forms when she arrived. Clothing was put in place shortly after.

Trin smiled as Niida poured the tea. "Busy day?"

"Very. Dorothea had to leave early. Her daughter is approaching her first shift, so they are watching her around the clock."

Trin sipped at the tea and sighed in relief. She really didn't like coffee. "Eagle, right?"

"Right. It is going to want to fly, and they have to help her control it." Niida sighed. "I thought it was tricky to learn to use four paws."

Trin smiled. "I wish I could say I understood, but..."

"Right. Of course."

That seemed to have garnered the attention of the ladies gossiping. One by one, they turned to look at her. Trin nibbled a sandwich and raised her brows. "Yes?"

One of the older women sneered, "Human? They let humans in here?"

Niida frowned. "Of course. She is a protected species."

Trin chuckled that Niida didn't mention that Trin owned the shop. It was best to figure out what they were dealing with.

The woman drummed her fingers on her table. "How can you even get through the day? You are feeble and weak."

Trin smiled. "I am also clever and good with my hands. You are Lady Meshnal?"

The woman blinked. "Yes. How do you know me?"

"I helped Lord Meshnal last week. His vehicle was stalled. He had blown a hose. He was late for dinner with you and showed me the gift he had purchased for your birthday."

The woman blinked. "He said he had vehicle trouble and that a young man had stopped to help him."

Trin grinned. "I was wearing trousers and a cap. It was drizzling, and I hate getting a good dress wet."

The woman didn't know what to say. It was scandalous that Trin had been wearing a set of trousers, but it was worse that she had helped a shifter in need. She was good and evil all wrapped up in one human package.

Trin continued to eat her way through the tray. "So, Niida, are you going to the shower on the weekend?"

"Of course. Wild horses couldn't keep me away. How do you think she is feeling?"

Trin smiled. "I think she will feel better for having us there."

"Did you want a ride?"

"No, I am going with Tobias and the portable machine. It is part of the gift." She winked.

"Are you nervous?" Niida was aware that their conversation was being listened to by eager ears.

"Nope. We are there for her. She needs us." Trin winked and sipped more tea.

"She does?"

Trin nodded. "Trust me on this. She definitely needs to see faces that don't want anything from her aside from her coming through the pregnancy healthy and happy."

Niida agreed. "Then that is what we shall be. I am hoping that she will be there for me when my time comes."

Trin blinked. "You too?"

"I am not showing yet, but yeah. About two months along."

Trin got up and hugged her. "Congratulations."

Niida laughed. "You are going to be an aunty."

Trin bit her lip. "I am going to have to think up an amazing gift."

Niida hugged her again. "Yes, you will."

Trin sat back down and finished her meal, watching the other groups leave. She helped Niida wash up and close up, walking arm in arm with her down the street. They met Brenner on the way to the Dexom home, and he took over the escort duty for his wife. Trin congratulated him on the infant in development, and he blushed. They had known each other since they were four months old. This was one secret that he had kept, and she didn't blame him. If Niida was confident enough to tell her about the baby, the couple was ready to share it. Trin would hope for the best for them. Every baby deserved to start off in a home filled with love, and they deserved to be wanted. In the Dexom home, they would have both.

Chapter Two

Trin sat next to Creata and laughed as she opened the gift. Tiny tools were crafted and laid out on a leather roll.

Creata laughed in delight. "Oh, wow. The kitchen appliances will be in danger as soon as the baby can walk."

The rest of the gift, the quilts, cloths, and diapers were sitting nearby, but Creata was holding up the small, functional tools one by one.

Creata's mother-in-law cleared her throat. "Dear, the ladies gathered here have also brought gifts. You might want to look at the presents they have brought."

Creata regretfully put the tools back and rolled them up. "Thank you, Trin. I love everything."

"You are welcome; I will be nearby once this gift orgy is over." She winked and kissed Creata on her cheek.

Once she surrendered the giving seat, one of the very posh ladies took her spot. Creata smiled politely and took the new gift.

Niida was standing to one side, sipping coffee from an elegant cup. "She loved the tools."

Trin chuckled. "She always did. If she hadn't met and mated with the Secretary to the Senator, I think she would have made an amazing mechanic."

Creata's husband was one of the most influential men in the country and one of the most powerful in the city. He had the ear of the senator and the love of his wife.

Niida snickered. "Speaking of mechanics, I think Tobias is having trouble with the portable unit."

Trin sighed and turned, walking past some of the young ladies who had to attend Creata's baby shower because her husband, Vasic Tal, secretary to the senator, was important. They were muttering about being stuck at this low-class bitch's shower. Trin paused but kept moving. She could make a scene later.

Tobias was dealing with the lineup of women by flirting and serving them standard coffee. She didn't speak to him. She moved around and took charge of the machine, spun some wheels, and let out a burst of steam. It was working in a minute.

Tobias gave her a happy glance, and she left to get some snacks at the buffet.

She was just reaching for a cluster of carrot sticks when she was slammed into from behind.

"What the hell?" She whirled and saw the young woman who was dripping with cranberry juice and glaring at her.

"You have ruined my dress!" Her high-pitched shriek got everyone to turn.

Trin tried to keep calm, but something about this woman set her on edge.

"You ruined your own dress. You cost me some carrot sticks." Her voice was a growl, and the sound startled her.

The woman was wearing a soft yellow gown that sported a brilliant red stain. She lifted her chin. "I should have expected someone of your sort here. After all, the pregnant cow is lowborn. Her friends are worse."

A glance in the direction the woman was speaking showed Creata standing within earshot. Trin snapped. She reached out and gripped the woman by the neck, shoving her head down and forward, pushing her out the room and through the open patio doors. In the back yard, Trin gave a hard shove.

"You don't know who you are dealing with, you human bitch!" The woman hissed.

Trin looked at her and watched her face scale over. "A dragon. Great. Shouldn't you know better than to attack a registered human?"

The woman hissed again and spoke in a weird gurgle. "When I am done with you, no one will know what you were."

The woman's eyes glowed, and she exhaled a pulse of energy.

Trin heard laughter, and someone shouted as she was thrown backward. Her dress flared around her, and she landed in a shrub.

Fury built up in her blood, and she stood and faced her opponent. Her fingers flexed, and she stretched her neck. "Really? You want to play?"

The shift to full dragon was taking a while. Trin moved forward, but it wasn't her taking the steps. Something was taking over, and it was mad.

Trin was watching from behind her own eyes as her dress tore and she was wrapped in ice and fire. She was tall. She was huge. Her limbs were long and tipped with talons, and her opponent was small. Half her size or smaller. Trin wasn't done shifting yet.

The woman—the other dragon—was staring at her in shock. Trin leaned back her scaled neck, and she roared to the heavens. A burn of fire and ice shot from her throat, and it formed a pillar above her that speared through the sky.

She looked back at the small topaz dragon, and it bowed low, placing its head down and belly to the ground. The signs of surrender were unmistakable.

Trin reached out and flicked the smaller dragon aside. She had made her point.

Niida's voice came to her from a distance. "Trin? Is that you?"

Trin looked over and walked slowly and carefully through the gardens. She looked at her friend and inclined her head. Her dragon wanted to fly, but there was no way that Trin was up for that.

"Did you know about this?" Niida waved at her body.

Trin slowly shook her head.

"Can you shift back?"

Trin shook her head again.

There was more of a commotion from inside the house, and constables poured out, stopping short when they saw her.

She stepped back and looked at them. Her dragon wanted to snack on them, but Trin said no.

One of the constables looked at her and told her to shift. She shook her head.

The piezoelectric charge struck her in the chest, so she swatted the constable that had the nerve to shoot her.

She felt the spines on her back lifting and dropping in agitation.

More men came. Trin's dragon scowled. They should not be there. They did not belong there. The men were wearing dark suits, and they sent the constables away.

Trin looked at the men, and her dragon was happy. They were dragons. Each of them. All four of them were dragons, and they were staring.

The first to walk up to her spoke in soothing tones. "Hello, miss. We are just going to take care of your catalyst, and then, we will be back to deal with you."

Trin sat down on her haunches, and then, she lay down with her forelegs folded and her head stretched along the grass. She took up a lot of space.

Creata walked up, against her mother-in-law's orders, and stroked Trin's nose. "I guess this was lurking behind those mad skills."

Trin snorted softly. She wasn't ready to commit to the reality of being a dragon. Her pregnant friend was an excellent way to calm down. She couldn't be irritated with Creata there.

The other dragoness was escorted off the premises. Only two of the dragon males returned to her.

One of the males was quite nice. He came up to her and murmured, "This must have been very confusing for you. Changing so suddenly. You are a beauty."

She blinked slowly. A beauty was not

something she would classify herself as. Not in human form anyway. She was blissfully normal in human form.

He stroked her scales, and she could feel his energy along her skin. It made her all warm and tingly inside.

The other dragon was just acting as supervisor. She was guessing if she got out of hand, he would shift and put her down.

The man touching her stroked his way down her neck and over to her flank. She felt a sharp pinch, which made her head whip toward him. He was standing there with a long tube in his hand. He had dosed her with something.

Trin tried to remain conscious, but her head spun, and a fog rolled across her thoughts. When she had a thought, it was that she had been knocked out by the pretty one.

Damnit.

* * * *

A crystal dragon. *Holy shit.* Brommin Artur Lefarge stared at the beast that was taking up the back garden of the Tal residence. The lady of the house was very concerned when Miss Mornith had picked a fight. She had called her husband, who had summoned the Track and Restrict agents in the area. The local constabulary had also been called, but they left when Brommin had taken charge of the scene.

What a scene it was.

Female dragons never grew to the size of males. They were mate dependant, for the most part, counting on their mate for protection. The dragon in the Tal's back garden was at least thirty-five feet long. She was lithe, and her skin was reflective and faceted.

He asked the homeowner. "Why hasn't she shifted back?"

The pregnant lady frowned in concern. "She isn't a dragon. She is a registered human."

The smaller white dragon was on her belly and grovelling. That would be Miss Mornith. She was all mouth and no brains.

Brommin sighed and reached into his long coat. "Right. Stay back. New shifts can be dangerous."

The lady of the house nodded. "I understand that."

He stepped forward and spoke softly

to the new dragon. "Hello, miss. We are just going to take care of your catalyst, and then, we will be back to deal with you."

He didn't know how she would take that, but she settled down and lay on her belly, watching them remove Miss Mornith.

He spotted a motion to his left, and the lady of the house passed him, stepping right up to the recumbent dragon. To Brommin's horror, she touched the huge head that lowered toward her.

She spoke softly to her friend and stroked her huge head.

The lady gave him a look, and he casually walked along her length, murmuring, "This must have been very confusing for you. Changing so suddenly. You are a beauty."

She was very relaxed with her friend speaking to her, so he ran his hand along the tough skin to her flank. She occasionally turned her head toward him, but the lady of the house had nerves of steel and kept her attention facing forward.

He slipped the injector out of the pocket of his leather greatcoat, and as carefully as he could, he activated it against her rear haunch, and the slight hiss got her attention.

She turned to look at him again, cocking her head as the strong sedative hit her system. Immobilizing a dragon's wings and hind end kept them grounded. From there, she should return to her human form as she was sedated.

The lady of the house kept stroking her friend's head as she slowly closed her eyes and her breath evened into the heaving bellows of a sleeping dragon.

As the dragon slowly shrank, the lady of the house called for a wrap.

Brommin murmured, "What do you mean a—oh."

When the dragon energy had dissipated, the woman left lying on the ground was definitely naked. Long, smooth limbs and a cascade of white and silver hair got his attention. She was lying on her belly so that was all he could see.

A woman with a concerned expression on her face brought a covering and put it over the sleeping woman. "This is going to piss her off. She loved having brown hair."

The lady of the house smiled. "Yeah, that is probably going to be the thing that upsets her most, not turning into a forty-foot dragon at my baby shower."

They tucked the blanket around her, and the other woman looked up at him. "What happens to her now?"

Brommin blinked. "She goes to the wheel, and she will be assessed by counsellors. If she is truly a dragon and not a weird mage or something, she will be trained and brought into our society."

The other woman frowned. "When can we visit her?"

The woman of the house nodded. "Right. When can we visit?"

"You can apply to the wheel for visitation. I am sure they will grant a few minutes in a week or so."

He bent down and picked up the shockingly light woman. "By the way, what is her name?"

The pregnant woman smiled. "Trin. I am sure she will tell you all she wants you to know when she wakes."

He nodded. "Thank you. Please excuse my departure, but there is a crowd gathering outside."

He held the pale-haired woman against his chest, and he opened his wings. The slide of leather against his emerging appendages was sensual and familiar. It wasn't something he would admit to, but it was his favourite part of emergency flight.

His second-in-command was examining what he could see of the woman, but he got his wings out as well, and with the flare of his silver wings, they bent and launched into the air a few seconds apart.

They had the first unregistered dragon in four decades with them. This was going to make some headlines. She was an amazing beast.

Chapter Three

Having had a hangover a time or two in her life, Trin knew it when she found her eyeballs trying to burn their way through the back of her skull.

"This is not my nightgown." She sat up and looked down at the frilly and lacy tube that encased her. She preferred sleeping in a chemise. Getting cold in the night was never a problem.

She tried to remember the events of the afternoon. She could remember seeing Creata, glowing and happy in the late stages of pregnancy. She remembered fixing the coffee machine, going for some food, and then, her brain was blank.

That is when I began to speak to you.

She paused. "I heard that."

I hope so. I have slept for so long I thought you would never let me wake. It is fortunate that the rude topaz was at the party to wake me.

Trin had no idea how to answer that. A soft knock at her door preceded the door opening.

"Miss? I was told to bring you a tray but leave it if you were still asleep."

Trin scooted up against the headboard. "I am awake."

The young woman nodded and flicked the stand out of the tray she was carrying. Once the legs were locked down, she set it over Trin's lap.

Trin smelled coffee and sighed. "Right. Coffee."

"It is standard here for breakfasts. Would you prefer tea?" The young woman smiled.

"Yes. How long have I been here?" Trin waited for the answer. She thought it was a day, but there was something wrong with the feel of her nightgown.

"This is the fourth day since you were brought here. You made it onto the news." The maid grinned.

"Four days? Damn. I have to get to the shop. Tobias will have killed the machine by now."

The young woman's eyes widened when Trin put the breakfast to one side and got to her feet. She swayed slightly but stiffened her limbs.

"Um, miss, you can't leave. You are under investigation by the senate. They want to know where you came from."

"Great. When can I talk to them? I just want to go home."

She turned and caught a glimpse of herself in the mirror. "What the hell happened to my hair?"

She walked up to the bureau and stared at the image. Her hair was still long, but instead of her very normal brown hair and brown eyes, her hair was now white with thick silver streaks, and her eyes had darkened to black.

The maid cleared her throat. "I cannot answer your questions. I will send someone in."

The woman was gone in a heartbeat. Trin went to the door the maid escaped through, and it was locked. She turned back and looked at the tray. If she couldn't get out, she may as well eat.

Everything on the tray was gone except the porcelain and cutlery. She had located the lav and brushed her hair before braiding it into a thick cable. A search of the room didn't yield any more clothing, and while she didn't have many social restrictions in her daily activities, she drew the line at walking the streets in her nighty.

She went to the window, and the leaded glass didn't offer her any escape. She was high. Very high. The spire. That was the only structure that was that tall in the city. She had literally been changed into the lady in the tower. If she tried to leave in her new form, dragons would be after her before she passed the city limits.

Trin paced back and forth in the small space, and when a knock on the door warned of another incoming visitor, she kept pacing.

"Miss Trin?"

She smiled. No one had gotten her name. "Yes?"

"I have some bloodwork to draw for the alchemist. Are you willing to have it done?"

The woman was wearing an apron pinned to the front of her blouse and skirt. Her sleeves were rolled up.

"Are you a doctor?"

The woman smiled. "I am Dr. Dredock, the alchemist. It has been decades since there was an unrecorded dragon."

Trin grimaced. "As far as you know."

The doctor raised her brows. "You are correct. May I draw some blood?"

"Sure." She walked over and sat

down on the edge of the bed.

The doctor prepped her instruments and glanced over. "Those who were there say that you were crystal. Clear and untouched by colour."

"So, I have been told. Now that my beast is awake, she is lecturing me on how beautiful and strong she is."

The doctor cleaned her skin and inserted the needle near her inner elbow. "Is the dragon form hereditary?"

"No idea. I am not close with my family." It was an understatement. Trin had no idea who her family was.

"Oh? What is your family name?" The doctor smiled as she took a second vial.

"Lem."

The doctor froze. "You are an orphan?"

"Yes."

The doctor put a small piece of gauze down, and she pulled the needle away. "Press down."

"Yes, Ma'am."

"What is your given name?"

Trin smiled. "I have an assigned name. Is that good enough?"

"Um, yes. For the samples."

Trin sighed and blurted it out. "Adolla Venatrin Lem. Raised at the Home for the Unknown, birthed by a woman struck by a vehicle at the side of the road. I don't know her name or my name."

The doctor paused. "That is a lot of information."

Trin snorted. "I thought that I would be asked it eventually, so I am getting used to the answer. This might curtail a bit of repetition."

The doctor smiled and pulled a small, flat container with crystals out. She placed the small glass container on the bureau, and she held up the syringe. "Just a little preliminary test to check on your power level."

Trin nodded and watched from a few feet away as the doctor took the syringe and let a drop fall into the crystals.

The flash and explosion sent the doctor spinning against the wall, and Trin ended up curled to one side as the jet of heat and power burned through the bureau, setting it on fire.

She heard shouts, and fire suppression was sprayed on the experiment. Hands grabbed her and pulled her upright, she heard someone shouting at her, but her ears were still ringing.

Dr. Dredock stood up and pressed a bleeding hand to her forehead. "It wasn't her. She's definitely a crystal dragon. She's pure energy, and I think that while we start running our tests, she needs to learn what she is. She needs a tutor."

Trin looked up, and she blinked at the familiarity of the man holding her with her arms back. He had been one of the four called to Creata's house. All of the dragons who had been there were tall and strapping. Having never properly met a dragon before, she wasn't sure if it was because it was en- demic to the type of shifter they were, or if these men had been chosen for the job.

Trin could see that his gaze wasn't fixed on her face; she looked down and saw the white muslin had been rendered nearly transparent in the spray of the fire retardant. Her breasts were outlined, nipples prominent. Trin scowled, and she whipped her head back, cracking him in the jaw. "Manners, asshole."

He let go of her upper arms, and she staggered forward. Another one of the responders took off his jacket and wrapped it around her. He winked at her. "Nice shot."

She could smell his scent and that of his mate. There was also the trace of children on the coat. She winked in return and said, "Practice."

He chuckled. "You can step back, Torm. She didn't do it. It was the good doctor who made the explosion."

Trin looked back over her shoulder, and the male she had struck was still clutching his jaw.

The doctor intervened. "She is definitely a crystal dragon. It was my own doubt that made me do the test in here. She will need a new room, clothing, and an instructor, as I said earlier. She is definitely a dragon. No mage could have put that much power into their blood."

Now that she had repeated herself, the men in the room paid attention to the alchemist. Trin felt a chill and looked over her shoulder. The leaded window that she had been staring out of was gone, as were several feet of brick.

The kindly guard beckoned to her. "We will get you a new bedchamber, and Sosa is already working on the clothing."

She looked to the doctor, and Dr. Dredock nodded. "Sormin is a good guy. Sormin, I need to speak with the senator. Could you help me arrange it?"

The dragon inclined his head. "It will be my honour as soon as I get Miss Trin settled in her new quarters."

She smiled. "I appreciate that. I am a little in need of some proper clothing."

"Then, we shall not hesitate. Please, come with me." He offered her his arm.

Trin pulled his coat on more firmly and took his arm. "Anywhere that doesn't have a plunge to my death next to my bed. I am not fussy."

He nodded and gave the younger dragon a glare. "Come with us."

The younger dragon ducked his head and followed.

The inner halls of the tower were narrow, and everyone was in human form to save space. It was a bit of a relief that etiquette won over shifter inclination in the heart of the government block.

They went up three levels before Sormin stopped and opened a door. "Here you are, Miss. I will have Sosa bring you the clothing when she has it."

She nodded and blushed. "Oh, here is your jacket. Thank you for the loan."

"You are most welcome, Miss." Sormin bowed.

Torm bowed as well. "Apologies, Miss."

She subtly pulled her nightgown away from her. "Right. No harm done. Have a fun day."

Torm blushed. "I will be outside your door if you need anything."

She blinked. "I am under guard?"

Sormin smiled slightly. "Just one guard until you are confirmed, Miss. I will find Sosa."

Trin nodded and waved farewell as she closed her door. When she turned around, she gasped. The room she was in was three times the size of the first one.

She looked around for a moment, made sure she wasn't being observed, and she ran toward the four-poster bed, shrieking and laughing as she jumped on it. Torm might have opened the door to check on her, but she didn't care. This was the first time in her adult life that she had been in a bed with a ceiling high enough to jump on.

Trin flopped on the bed and tried not to worry about the shop. She was sure that Brenner had taken charge when Ni-ida had told him what happened.

It was nice to have friends and business partners she could trust, but she still wondered if anyone was checking on Tobias. She had a business to take care of after all.

Chapter Four

Dr. Dredock paced outside the senator's private office. She was nervous about the information but was sure that it had to be shared quickly.

When the guard opened the door and let her in, she smiled briefly and headed into the dragon senator's inner sanctum.

Senator Lefarge greeted her with a smile. "Doctor, I hear that you requested an audience."

"Yes, Senator." She bobbed a short curtsy.

"Please, have a seat."

She stepped forward and eased into

the leather seat. "Thank you, sir. I am here to speak on behalf of the new dragon."

He twisted his pen in his fingers. "You mean the new arrival."

"No, sir. She is a new dragon. She has power and a beast but none of the training that goes with it. She might be able to fly, she might not. From what her friend Niida said when I spoke to her this morning, Trin has never been exposed to another dragon. If you do things normally, she will not react as expected. She has the reflexes of a street fighter and the impulses of a survivor. If you are planning to send her out on a mate-selection flight, she is more likely than not to attack them in self-defense." She took a deep breath.

He frowned. "So, if we enforced the

enclave's regulations..."

"She will run or fly. She will escape."

The senior dragon nodded and tented his fingers for a moment before straightening. "What would you recommend?"

"Educate her. She is smart, crafty, and quite reasonable. She has offered up bits of her past, knowing that we would pursue them." She folded her hands in her lap. "Give her every bit of information you would give to one of your own family. All the histories and horrors, all the laughters and stupidities. If you can do that, you will gain her cooperation in planning her future."

He caught on to what she had said. "What about her past?"

"Her last name is Lem." That said it all as far as Dredock was concerned.

The senator froze. "Lem? As in the

name given to foundlings?"

"Correct. She can't tell you about her family because she doesn't know. She has never met a dragon until this incident. She is entering a foreign land, and she has no way out of it."

He exhaled. "Thank you for this information. It will change what I had in mind."

She nodded. "I have her name and where she was raised if that is of any use."

"Give it to Vasic and have him get everything he can on her."

"Yes, sir." She got up, curtsied again, and left the room, breathing freely when she was leaning against the door on the safe side with the heavily armed guards.

She straightened and walked to the desk of the senator's private secretary.

Vasic Tal was a lion, but in a tower filled with dragons that didn't mean he was in charge.

"Secretary Tal?"

He looked up from his work and smiled. "Yes, Dr. Dredock?"

"I have been charged with giving you the identity of the new dragon in our midst. The senator would like you to look into her."

He nodded. "Of course. What is the name?"

"Adolla Venatrin Lem. Raised at the Home for the Unknown."

He jotted the information down. "Thank you. I will do the research. You have met her?"

"I have. She has a quick wit."

"Yes. She does." Vasic nodded and smiled. "She is also fiercely loyal."

He paused, and Dr. Dredock began to remember whose house the new dragon had been found at. "You know her?"

"I will get the report to the senator as soon as I am able. Thank you for your help. By the way, never call her Adolla. She really hates it."

He turned and began to dial the phone with steady concentration. Dr. Dredock knew a dismissal when she saw one.

She walked out of the executive wing and down to her lab. She had tests to run on the blood she had drawn, and if she was lucky, she might be able to pin down a little bit of Trin's lineage. Power signatures were distinctive. Someone, somewhere, had to have had similar levels on record.

* * * *

The knock on the door brought Trin to full alert. When the door opened and Sosa came in with armloads of bags and boxes, Trin ran forward to help.

"Did you buy out the store?"

"No, I raided the storeroom. I am not trying to be rude, but you are very tall for a female dragon." Sosa smiled.

"Is Sormin your sibling?"

Sosa blinked. "He is. Well spotted. Most who are near us for the first time think that we are spouses."

"You smell different. It is weird. At the shop, we had the walls lined and an air-handling system designed to reduce the scents from outside and minimize the overpowering smell of the coffee. Scent was always something to be removed, but now, I can see the appeal. I can learn a lot about someone just by smelling them."

Sosa laughed. "We call it scenting, but I understand what you mean."

"Sormin smells like his wife and child. I would never have picked up on that before today." Trin rubbed the back of her neck. "So, what did you bring me?"

"Standard dragon clothing. If you can grab a shower, it would be helpful."

Trin knew a dismissal when she heard one. She headed for the bathroom and took a quick shower, still jumping when she saw her hair in the mirror. That was going to take a while to get used to.

The faucets got her attention as she turned them on. She could almost visualize the mechanism that was in action, turning and allowing water from the lower level to be pumped up. She dropped her nightgown and stepped under the warm cascade.

As delightful as the shower was, she made it fast. Real clothing was waiting for her beyond the door, including shoes.

She wrapped thick towels around her hair and body and pattered back into the bedroom. Three different outfits were waiting for her, and they all made her want to dive back into the shower.

She looked over Sosa's shoulder and grimaced. "What are those?"

"They are gowns that will fit you. We will have to go to a seamstress to get dragon gowns made for you."

Trin blinked. "Dragon gowns?"

"Unlike other beings, we travel quite a distance when we shift. We cannot be guaranteed clothing when we land, so with propriety in mind, we have hired mages to create clothing that shifts with us."

"Mages? We have mages in the city?" Channelled magic was a human skill. As a rule, the city didn't allow mages to walk the streets.

"They are licensed and monitored. We have four mage seamstresses in the city, and they work almost exclusively for the dragons." Sosa smiled. "So, pick your poison. Yes, they are all very frilly."

Trin looked over the gowns, and she bit her lip. "Nothing with trousers?"

"Oh, no. Not for dragons."

"What if I want trousers? I like a

split-front gown with leggings under it." Trin had made up her mind in an effort to find something to wear, but she wanted to be clear with her new companion that this wasn't going to be her standard for moving around.

"You will have to get the council to allow it."

Trin frowned. "Why?"

Sosa looked at her in surprise. "Your clothing is dictated by the council. As a dragon female, you must be easily identifiable at all times."

Trin blinked. "I quit."

"You can't quit. This is what you are."

Trin crossed her arms. "I wasn't *this* last week."

Sosa blinked. "Ah. Right. I keep forgetting. Have you chosen a dress?"

Trin scowled. "I will wear it today, but as soon as I can get my regular wardrobe back, I am going to be wearing it."

Sosa gave her a bland look. "We will see."

Trin pointed at the rich blue dress. It would be flattering with her new colouring, and the mandarin collar was one that she preferred. It had minimal lace frothing on it, so it was the lesser of the three evils.

Sosa nodded and handed her a chemise. Trin pulled the fabric over her head, and as it dropped into place, she pulled her towel free. Next came the undergarment, and finally, the corset was wrapped around her.

She grunted as she worked the laces. Normally, she wore clothing that had exterior support. Corsets were a necessary part of life in the twenty-first century.

"You do that very well."

Trin gave her a look. "I have never had someone else in the room while I am dressing. I do this on my own."

When she had tied off and tucked the laces, she tugged the corset into an even setting. The petticoats went on over that, and when she was ready, Sosa brought the dark fabric to her.

Sosa lifted the dress above her head, and Trin slid her arms into the sleeves. The rest was a flurry of tugging and fluffing.

The buttons up the back guaranteed that she was going to have good posture for the rest of the day. Her hands smoothed over the silk, and she kept them from forming fists.

"Now, we just need to attend to your hair." Sosa looked her over.

"I've got it. Just a moment." Trin walked into the bathroom again, and she winced at the puff that the shower had made of her hair. She looked like a dandelion. With quick strokes, she pulled her hair back in a ponytail and from there, a few twists brought it back in a bun, and with one hand, she searched for pins. When her search didn't find anything, she came out and spoke to Sosa. "Where are the pins?"

"You don't pin your hair. Well, not until you are married. If you will allow me?"

She sighed and let the tight ball unravel. "Go for it."

Sosa got the brush from the bathroom, walked up behind Trin and quickly loosened the ponytail, flipping the ends through it at the base of her skull before making another tail and doing the same, crafting a ladder effect down her back.

"There. Simple yet elegant. It is very striking against the dark silk. Good choice." Sosa nodded.

Trin grimaced. "Great. Are there shoes?"

Trin would have preferred her normal and very practical boots, but the short lace-up versions matched the design of the dress. Her toes were slightly pinched, but otherwise, the fit was good.

She stood straight as Sosa walked around her and gave her a frank assessment. "The dress is too wide in the waist, but since we are on the way to the seamstress, it will be taken care of."

"Are we going now?"

"Of course. Our escort is waiting." Sosa gestured to the door.

Trin inhaled and exhaled slowly. "Right. Let's go."

Sosa nodded and opened the door. "We are ready. Let's go."

Trin didn't even look at her reflection. Her appearance didn't matter. Her life had spun out of her control, and it wasn't going to come to a halt any time soon. She may as well ride the cyclone.

Chapter Five

Four guards were a little much, but the karros that they drove was just right. It had six doors, was a muted pewter, and had an elegant shape that she appreciated.

The vehicle purred through the streets in near silence. Trin didn't ask any questions, she just watched and smiled as the familiar signage of Harbinger Coffee and Tea appeared when they rounded the corner. The line was outside and heading down the block, but folk were leaving the shop at a good pace. It was a relief. She might be close to being under arrest, but her business was continuing on. Brenner would be delighted.

When they arrived at the shop, two of the guards exited and one restrained Trin with a hand on her arm until the shop had been cleared.

Trin snorted. "Right. Like anyone knows who I am."

Torm pulled a tablet out of his jacket pocket, and he queued up a news article. He handed it to her. "The attendants of the party appear to have spilled their experiences in the press."

She took the tablet and read of her brutal attack on the shy and delicate dragon who was only defending the pregnant lioness. "Well, hell. I can only imagine that Creata is having either a good laugh or a lot of stress. Either way,

I need to go and visit her."

Torm gave her an astonished look. "You can't associate with other shifters. It isn't appropriate."

She tensed and looked at him. "Are you telling me that I can't associate with one of my oldest and dearest friends? Fuck this. To hell with this."

Trin darted for the door, and when Torm grabbed her wrist, she twisted her hand and raked her nails across his arm. He let go with a hiss, and she was out of the karros.

The skirts tangled in the vehicle's door, and she was slowed enough for two of her guards to flank her. Sormin sighed. "We will take Torm off your detail. His tendency to grab you is becoming awkward. I have called for a replacement. Now, please, come with me."

Sormin offered her his arm, and with Sosa watching nervously, she took it.

Torm was getting first aid from the driver. There was blood outside the vehicle.

Trin checked her nails, and they were pearl white and diamond hard. They also had skin under the nails. "Huh, that is new."

Sormin sighed. "As many parts of you as can manage it will begin to exhibit dragon characteristics. The hair and eyes are the first then the nails, and soon, your skin will take on a pearly sheen."

"Why do you look normal or at least nearly human?" Trin murmured as they entered the shop.

"I am not a crystal dragon. Your body

is power and energy for a new genera-tion. You have to contain it."

Trin snorted. "Yeah. I hope there is a manual for that because I am not doing so well today."

"You have only attacked two dragons and both assaulted you first. There were proper witnesses to both incidences, no matter what the tabloids say."

"This is fucking confusing."

He chuckled and patted her hand in a paternal manner. "For you, I can under-stand that it is a new world. I am sure that the senator is working on steps to make it easier for you."

She shrugged. "I can't wait for this to get easier. There are so many more things that I would rather be doing than playing dress-up."

There was comfort in the dress shop.

When the proprietor came toward her, Trin smiled. "Hello, Mirbella."

Mirbella Montague, seamstress extraordinaire, came toward her with a gliding step and a huge smile. "Trin Lem! I had no idea that you were my high-profile client. Why didn't you tell me you were a dragon?"

Trin took her hands and squeezed them gently. "I didn't know until this week. So, can I get some fancy new clothing made in the styles I like?"

Mirbella flicked looks at Trin's entourage. "I will run it by the council. They like their females to be identifiable at a glance."

"I can understand that, but there is comfort to consider. Perhaps a similar silhouette, but the open skirt, trousers, and boots?"

"I think that I can make it happen. Their concern has never been with what is under the clothing, just the style."

Sosa cleared her throat. "You two have met?"

Mirbella inclined her head. "When Miss Trin deigns to get clothing made, she comes to me. I enjoy the challenge. I am going to enjoy this one even more. I will get to make ball gowns and put her in them. I have dreamed of that for five years."

Trin chuckled, Sosa smiled wryly as if she should have known that Trin had been there before, and the ladies all sat around looking at pattern books and eating cakes while Mirbella made suggestions.

After two hours of chatter, debate, and colour selections, Trin was wearing a new dress with businesslike lines in deep blue with thick silk. The silhouette was narrower than it had been, and Sosa looked surprised at how the more simple style made Trin stand and look. Her entire bearing was changed with a few metres of cloth and a good cup of tea.

Mirbella proffered the charge plate, and while she winced at the number, Trin paid it without hesitation.

Sosa stared. "The council was going to pay for that."

Trin smiled. "I know. If I pay for it, I have more say in the end product. Mirbella knows what I like and knows the regulations that the dragons have set down. She will find the middle ground that satisfies us both."

Sormin grinned. "You are very clever."

"I am not a child. I am not a teenager going through the first shifts. I am an adult woman who has lived her own life. Twenty-five percent of my life is behind me. I remember every moment of it, and no one was there picking out my clothing." Trin gave Sormin the arch of her brows.

He inclined his head. "You are correct. You cannot be treated as a new dragon. I will bring your concerns to the senator. I am sure he will accept the effort that you are making."

"Right. Well, what is next? I noted that you and the others on guard duty didn't have anything to eat. Would you like to grab a wrap? There is a great shop just around the corner."

He paused. "Literally around the corner?"

Mirbella nodded. "It is where I get all my meals on the nights that I am working late."

Sormin looked at the other guard and grinned. "Well, if they are just around the corner, it would be a shame to miss this opportunity."

Trin nodded to Mirbella, linked arms with Sosa, and nearly beat Sormin to the door. He paused to brief the men outside, and Torm was pleasantly gone. The man who was standing in Torm's place was strangely familiar.

The pretty one. My pretty one. The dry rumble in her head was unmistakable. This man woke her dragon on sight. That was dangerous.

"Miss Lem. It is good to see you well and conscious." He bowed to her.

Sormin made the introductions.

"Miss Trin Lem, this is Brommin Lefarge, head of the Tactical Restraint Unit. He met you on the day of your emergence."

Trin tried not to blush. "I recall it. He stabbed me in the ass with a syringe."

Brommin grinned. "It was the upper thigh."

She wrinkled her nose. "I don't know. My awareness of my limbs was a little skewed."

"There is a thinning of the scale at the top of the hip. It was my only chance to get the sedative in."

Sormin chuckled. "You two can discuss the injection at leisure. Since we are done at this shop, our newest dragoness has suggested a shop around the corner for wraps."

Brommin nodded. "I could eat."

The other two guards nodded, and with a word to the driver, their party walked the two hundred metres to the shop.

Sosa was looking around with bright eyes. Trin slowly realized that her companion might never have been in a wrap shop before. She linked her arm with Sosa and hauled her to the front of the shop.

Sosa whispered, "I don't know what to order."

"Something light?"

Sosa nodded.

Trin ordered two salads with dressing and toasted flatbread. Sweet tea was ordered, and with a pass of her wrist over the payment plate, Trin took care of it.

"You have an implant?" Sosa blinked.

"Of course. I was not raised a dragon. This is part of living in the modern world." She chuckled and waited for the guards to order before she selected a defensible table. The attendants of the shop held out chairs for Trin and Sosa but then left quickly when the guards growled.

Brommin was on her right, and Sormin was on her left. Sosa was across from her, wedged between the other two.

Sosa looked at her and giggled. "This is fun. I have never eaten in a public establishment before."

Trin winked. "This is how I survived. I work and get something to eat on the way home then do it all again on the way to work."

Brommin chuckled and sipped at his

ice water. "You don't cook?"

"No. Do you?"

He paused. "Um, no. I actually don't."

"So, there you go. Cooking for myself is a luxury I haven't earned yet." She sat straight and clapped when the salad was set in front of her. She had ordered the same thing for her and for Sosa, so it didn't matter who got what.

The men got their food a moment later, and Trin lifted her fork. She didn't hesitate. She dove in.

Watching Sosa eat the salad lashed with sprinkles of shredded meat cast off from the huge cylinder that was rotating next to flames behind the counter was amazing and amusing at the same time. Sosa was on a voyage of discovery, and it was fun to watch.

Cucumber, yogurt, dill, and a dash of salt made up the dressing on the shredded greens with chunks of tomatoes facing upward. It was a light meal that fitted well with the dessert-first theme of the day.

The guards muttered as they ate their wraps. Trin smiled. The sounds were that of men who were happy with what they were gnawing on.

By the time Trin had crunched down the last mouthful, the guards were waiting, and their plates had been cleared.

Brommin asked, "Miss Lem, do you eat here often?"

"As often as I can. There is a great coffee place just down the lane as well. It is a lovely neighbourhood." She smiled brightly.

She folded her napkin on top of her

salad bowl, and it was soon whisked away.

She sipped at the tea until it was gone, and when she glanced around, happy dragons surrounded her. Good food worked with any shifter. They were all appetite motivated. Food, sex, family, their appetites were tremendous.

Brommin gave her a sly look. "You seem to know the neighbourhood well."

"Yes. I live up the block."

Sosa shook her head. "Not anymore. You live in the central tower until such a time as there is no longer a dragon senator."

Trin scowled. "We will see about that."

Brommin blinked slowly and grinned. "This is definitely going to be an interesting process. When we return to the hub, the senator would like to speak to you."

Trin swallowed but straightened her shoulders. "Right. Well, I suppose we should be going."

Brommin got to his feet and pulled her chair out as she stood. She moved to the side, gave a friendly smile and a wave to those who were working behind the counter, and then, she hiked outside where their karros was waiting for them.

She sat sandwiched between Brommin and Sormin as they pulled away from the shop and cruised down the laneway that contained the third shop in her tiny empire. She would be back in the shops soon, in one way or another. No one could keep her from her territory.

Chapter Six

Trin was escorted through the halls by Sormin and Brommin. She couldn't help but notice small groups of children aging from five to nineteen.

"Why are there so many children here?" She asked it of both of her escorts.

Brommin answered. "They are here for classes. We run dragon courses from the time they can read and write. For one month a year, the young dragons come here to learn about what it will mean to become one of the most powerful shifters in the world."

They passed through the tower, and to Trin's surprise, the senator's private offices were in the centre on the second floor.

Vasic was at the desk outside the two huge doors, which sported their very own guards.

She waved and inclined her head. "Lord Tal, how is Creata?"

"She is concerned for your safety and even talking back to my mother. I am glad to see you safe and looking well." He smiled, showing the slight hint of fang that he enjoyed keeping available. You never knew when you would have to bite someone.

Brommin blinked. "Right. I forgot. You know each other."

"Trin is my wife's oldest and dearest friend. She would be very upset if anything happened to Trin, and then, I would have to let her tear this place apart looking for her. Creata is an excellent tracker." He smiled brightly. "Oh, and your father is waiting for you."

Brommin sighed. "Right. Thanks for that subtle warning."

Trin grinned. "He was making a joke. It has taken him a while, but he is developing a sense of humour."

Sormin cleared his throat. "If you say so."

Trin was definitely light-hearted as they walked toward the huge doors. The guards nodded to Brommin, and they pulled the doors open.

The interior of the senator's chambers was wood panelled, dragon portraits were everywhere on the walls, and the ceiling was over twenty feet up. There was a lot of space in this space.

A man was sitting at the desk, and he was staring at her as she walked toward the single chair sitting in front of the polished black wood.

"Ah, Miss Trin Lem. Please, be seated."

She quirked her lips. He had obviously been warned about how she liked to be addressed. She moved around the chair, backed up until her limbs made contact through the layers, and she slowly sank into the seat.

Trin kept her hands folded demurely in her lap. She waited, and he stared at her. Eventually, he spoke.

"So, you have caused quite the stir around here." He tapped his pen on his desk.

"So, I am being given to believe." She

smiled politely.

"Congratulations on having a severe-ly strong dragon. The last crystal dragon was centuries ago."

She cocked her head. "What is the difference between a crystal dragon and a quartz dragon?"

His mouth opened slightly, which was a funny look for him. "You don't... right. Education will be the first thing to schedule for you."

She raised her eyebrows. "Are you saying I am ignorant?"

"No, simply uneducated in the ways of dragons. It will make things easier for you if you understand why we do what we do."

"That would be pleasant. Do you know why I am a dragon yet?"

He shook his head. "We are looking

into it."

"I hope you get farther than I did."

"You looked into your origin?" He was surprised again.

"Of course. Like anyone else, I wonder who my parents are. Well, I suppose most people know."

He nodded. "What do you know about your birth?"

She took a deep breath and faced him straight on. "My mother was in the late stages of pregnancy, and she was struck by a vehicle. I was born as she died. They took me to a hospital, and three days later, I was at the Home for the Unknown wearing the name I currently have. From all indications, my mother was not from this city, but she was walking toward it."

The senator leaned back. "You know

a lot, but do you know her identity?"

"No. There was none, and obviously, no father was in the picture as well." She shrugged. "It is a mystery that I no longer have time for."

He seemed surprised. "You don't wish to know your parents?"

"My mother is very dead, so if my father is alive, he has never looked for me. I don't mind, but I won't halt my life to find those answers."

"That is fair enough. Do you mind if I pursue it? I am very inquisitive."

Brommin let out a snort. The senator gave him a wry glance. "Ignore my son unless you are choosing him, but that will be decided by you at a later date."

She blinked and glanced at the drag-on on her left. "What?"

Brommin murmured, "A dragoness

of your power has the right to choose her mate."

She blinked and looked back at the senator. "Well, that is something. It won't be Torm. He is way too grabby."

Senator Lefarge scowled. "Grabby?"

"He has attempted to contain me twice. I am not appreciative." She smiled politely.

"I see. Brommin, were you aware of this?"

He nodded. "I was made aware earlier today. He was removed for medical treatment, and then, he will be contained until his rut fades."

Trin blinked. "Rut?"

The senator smiled grimly. "It is one of the things you are going to learn."

"Wonderful. When will that start?"

Senator Lefarge looked to Sormin.

"When can we get everything in place?"

"I will verify that Sosa is available to act as her companion, and it can begin tomorrow."

The senator smiled. "Excellent. Anything else?"

Brommin cleared his throat. "I believe that Miss Lem wishes to have autonomy regarding her clothing."

Senator Lefarge looked her over. "What she is wearing seems fine."

Trin twisted her lips. "I prefer a more functional daily style that is less restrictive. I am not a fan of lace, and petticoats irritate me."

The senator scowled. "I would need to see examples."

"I can call on Vasic for a reference as to my personal taste. The clothing will be more austere, but it will be more functional. That is what I am working toward."

He asked his son, "Everything is being made to transform?"

Brommin nodded. "It is."

"Then, until it becomes a problem, it is not a problem. She isn't a born dragoness, and she will be given the respect and choices for someone who has lived outside the protection of the council. Our ladies are given a uniform for the ease of seeing them in events. No one is going to mistake Trin Lem for anything other than Trin Lem."

Brommin smiled. "Correct, Senator."

"Excellent. Well, I hope to hear of your progress soon, Miss Lem. Welcome to our community."

She got to her feet and paused. "When can I check on my businesses?"

He tapped his pen. "Do you have someone who can bring you data?"

"I do. Can I write letters to him?"

"Or you could call. We have a Meucci for you when you are ready to make a call. Sormin has it."

Sormin pulled out the communication device and handed it to her.

"What happened to my shredded clothing? My Tesla unit was in there."

Brommin filled in. "The clothing was gathered by the household, so they probably have your unit. You can ask Vasic."

She nodded. "I will. When can I visit Creata? She is getting close to having her child."

Sormin cleared his throat. "They are lions. They are not on the list of protected homes for you to visit."

She looked to the senator, and she glared at him. He nodded shortly. "We will make the arrangements."

"Thank you. I have a number of friends out there in the city, and I am not young and stupid enough to be cowed into ignoring them." She nodded. "Was there anything else?"

The senator looked amused. "I believe you have covered enough for today."

"Excellent. Can I get a tour of this building?"

"Please. Brommin, Sormin, show her around. Brommin, don't forget to set up her education. Sormin, work on her guard detachment."

The men nodded, and Sormin led the way out of the office.

Vasic was at his desk, and Trin

walked up to him. "Lord Tal, I am authorized to ask if my Tesla was found in my personal effects after the transformation." She smiled brightly.

He nodded. "The effects were gathered together after the event, so I will take a look this evening."

"Thank you. I will pop by tomorrow."

He raised his brows. "You are staying?"

Trin shrugged. "I have to. I need to learn what I am and how to be a dragon. This is the best place to do it."

"Excellent. I will let Creata know where you are. She worries."

Trin inclined her head. "I know. Please give her a hug from me. I didn't mean to wreck her party."

He leaned forward. "She was relieved that it was over. All the presents, none of the chit-chat."

Trin giggled and bobbed a quick curtsey. She turned back to Brommin and Sormin. "Right. I guess I have had enough outside time today. Can I start studying?"

Sormin smiled. "I will bring you a primer that you can go over in preparation for beginning your studies tomorrow."

"Excellent. Let's go then." She nodded and walked down the hall that led to the main expanse.

Brommin moved swiftly and cut her off, offering her his arm.

She scowled but put her hand on the back of his wrist anyway, allowing him to lead her to the lift with Sormin walking behind them. At least Brommin hadn't pushed the issue. No one touched her without her permission. It was nice to see progress.

"Sosa, don't you have a mate yet?" Trin was brushing her hair out as she got ready for bed.

"No, Miss. Dragonesses don't go through the choosing process until they are twenty-five. That is when their dragon gets insistent."

Trin paused. "I am twenty-five."

Sosa paused while hanging up the gown Trin had worn. "Oh, I am sure your dragon will give you time."

"I am not so sure. She is rummaging around behind my eyes at all times, and I am not sure that it is a recent occurrence." She braided her hair over her shoulder and flicked the rope behind her.

"I am sure it is. Have you finished the primer?"

Trin looked at the picture book about the dragons and shifters coming to the new continent and making themselves at home. It was common knowledge, though she hadn't realized that the Lefarge dragons were descendants of the original fliers that carried the first settlers over to the rocky expanse.

"I have finished it. I have memorized the names of the original arrivals as well as the initial dissidents in Europe. Even the dates of the public exposure of the shifters during the inquisition are now burned into my memory."

Sosa smiled. "Excellent."

"So, Sosa, why are you here as a companion?"

"It is our duty to serve visitors and the nobles when they come to the tower. We even host folk from other cities."

Trin paused. "I have had a few customers from other cities. How do folks get out of the city?"

"You have to get a writ from the senator's office. Why do you ask?"

Trin smiled slightly. "The world is opening up to me. I am just wondering how far it can go."

Sosa nodded, but there was a worried look in her eyes as she left for the night.

Trin walked to the balcony and stared out at the night, her gown ruffling in the breeze. Tomorrow she would start becoming an educated dragon. The world had better watch out, her dragon had plans, and this city was just the beginning.

Chapter Seven

Trin walked with Sormin and a new guard, Irdol. Neither would answer when she asked about Brommin, but then, they weren't chatty today.

They went to the main floor in the lift, crossed the lobby, and then entered another lift. Sormin used a key, and the lift went down two levels.

The doors opened, and the smell of books, paper, and ink rushed in on her.

Sormin gestured for her to enter. "Your tutor is waiting. We will remain up top until he summons us."

"I am being left alone with a man?"

She was amused as it was a breach of protocol from what Sosa had told her.

"With the historian. If he tries anything, we are sure you will defend yourself accordingly." Sormin grinned. "Also, Sosa will be down in two hours. She has a meeting this morning."

"I did wonder why she rushed out. See you two later." She held her primer to her side and walked out of the lift, into the mosaic-covered entryway.

The doors to the lift closed behind her, and she didn't look back. She stepped forward with her skirts making the crisp sound of heavy silk. There was a table with a stack of books on it and a tea tray nearby with two cups situated on it.

She walked up to the table and looked at the books. History of dragons, geography of the continent, rules of deportment for dragons and other shifters. Yes, this was definitely her study stack.

She picked up the book on history and started to flip through the details of the reasons the shifters had left humanity and Europe behind.

Trin was past the second chapter when the shifters were defending themselves against religious oppression and making plans to fly west when she heard the scrape of a boot.

She glanced up and blinked. "Brommin?"

He smiled. "This is my normal assignment."

"You normally collect books for aging first-time dragons?" She watched as he set his collection of books down on the table next to the others. He was dressed in a proper suit instead of the black leather coat of the guards.

"No, I normally man the archive. I only work in the Tactics and Retrieval area when necessary. Fortunately, dragons only misbehave occasionally. It leaves more time for my studies."

He went to the tea tray. "Sugar or cream?"

"One sugar, please."

He set up their tea and carried the cups over, setting them down on the table. "Now, I am going to test you on your basic historical knowledge, and then, we will get into the particulars of the evolution of dragon society among the other shifter species."

She nodded. "Shall I have a seat?"

"Sit, stand, whatever you like. Are you ready to begin?"

She took a deep breath and set her book of history down. "I am ready."

"What year did the first magical inquisition begin?"

She cocked her head. "I believe it was Laguedoc in 1184."

He looked surprised. "Very good. Most put it in the thirteenth century."

She reached out and patted the book she had been reading. "I just learned that. First, they came for the mages, and the mages flushed out the shifters to save themselves."

He leaned back. "Go on."

"The shifters gathered together and discussed a way to leave the humans behind. The fastest dragons went exploring and came back with tales of a vast expanse of land with natives in some areas and wide-open spaces in others. They struck a deal to keep to their cities and only use enough land for their crops and beasts, and in turn, they promised to defend the locals when the Europeans descended en masse. When the settlers arrived as foretold, the shifters kept up their end of the bargain and drove the human settlers back to the sea."

"Excellent."

"Well, I did go to school in the city." She chuckled. "I learned the same things as all the shifters in my class."

He nodded and looked at the books he had selected. "Well, in that case, we will begin the details of the dragon coalition. Did you know that you are named after three of the founding dragons?"

That was a surprise. She had always

believed that she was simply named after a random selection of names. The Lem was a reference to her not having a proper family name, but the other two were surprising.

"I did not know that."

"Adolla was one of the explorers who found this continent. Years later, Venatrin was a dragon that bodily hauled the settler ships back to the ocean. She could summon the winds, and the Europeans were returned to their lands in a matter of days."

He paused for effect. "Adolla was a crystal dragon. She could hide while in flight and was able to cruise over human settlements with no one the wiser."

"I had no idea. I didn't even know the names of the dragons."

"Well, that is part of your education

now. You have a starting point." He pulled a book out and handed it to her. "This is a genealogy of the dragons going back as far as we have records."

She nodded and opened the book. "This goes back three thousand years."

"You only need to read it; I will test you for general understanding, and then, we will move on to etiquette. The history book you were reading can remain with you until you finish it."

Trin smiled. "Thank you. Right. I will get going on this. Can I wander around?"

"If that helps you read, it is fine. Do what you need to do." He smiled. "I will be puttering around and filing the monthly council reports."

"This may be rude, but does your father mind that you are an archivist?"

Brommin chuckled. "He finds it very useful when I can find precedents in a matter of minutes for nearly every occurrence. That is how he found one that allowed you to work around your personal style. It was a previous situation where a dragon had travelled here from another city and found a mate. Her style didn't match, and so, in order to keep her comfortable, a precedent was set."

She smiled. "So, the senator was warned about my wardrobe choices?"

"We do have communicators after all." He smiled. "It is the contribution that humans made to our society. There is a book on that as well."

She sighed and found her starting point in dragon history. It was time to study.

After two cups of tea and pacing for two hours, she finished the history, and her brain felt fuzzy. Dragons had been the heroes and villains of their own story for thousands of years and had recorded it all.

The dragons who had earlier risen against humanity had written down their motivations, and with only a few exceptions, they wanted to better the lot of the people in the area under the boot of the nobility. Dragons didn't hate all humans, just some select ones.

When she had gotten to her namesake, she had been surprised. Adolla had five children and a husband when she chose to make the exploration flight because only those with her speed and particular skills were suited to it. She forbade her children from following her, and that irritated them, but her husband stood by her on the day she took flight. He watched for her every day until she returned, and when she informed the council of the heading for the flight, he had the children start packing immediately.

Symran, the jet dragon, was a good and caring husband. When they made it to the new continent, he built their home, and eventually, they had three more children.

During the passage, Symran had carried an entire village on his back. Adolla had carried their children, and she had chosen the site of her home and the city they were currently living in. It was high, on stone, defensible and there were enough forests around to keep the other shifters happy.

Explaining to the locals that their people wore two forms had been tricky, but once the language barrier was worked through, the village explained their own history, which included strangers coming and turning their people into beasts.

That gave the dragons pause. They explained that it was the tradition for shifters to come to those of their blood and help to bring the beast out, to protect the change between human and animal.

A few examples later and a close bond had been made that now included an exchange of shifters and locals to increase understanding.

The rest of the history was dotted with human incursion into the new and safe land and minor territory skirmishes between dragons and shifter groups, which brought on the necessity for the councils. With the right to not only police their own kind, but also call on the dragons or others for help, the council system made things stable.

She closed the book and looked around. She had no idea where she had wandered to.

"Uh, Brommin?"

There was no reply for a moment, and then, she heard a voice from a distance. "Yes?"

"I have gotten lost near the collection of..." She looked around. "The erotic works of the lion shifters."

"I am on my way." There was laughter in his voice, and it took him five minutes to find her.

She sighed and walked toward him

when she saw him. "Thank you."

"No, thank you. Most start wander-ing toward my voice, and they get tan-gled in the stacks." He smiled. "Have you finished?"

"I have. Ready for my test."

"Sosa has joined us and has brought a tray of snacks. Why don't I quiz you during our break, and then, you can begin the etiquette rules and regula-tions? Now that you know where we have come from, the way we keep our-selves restrained will make more sense."

"I hope so. The more I see, the more the rules confuse me, but reading about the mixing of councils, it now makes sense."

He nodded and walked with her through the endless twists and turns of the archive.

As they neared Sosa, she asked, "Why is there a large collection of lion shifter erotica?"

He chuckled. "Their males are a little repressed by being around such competent and aggressive women. They break out and write stories about damsels in distress."

Sosa blushed slightly as she heard about their subject matter.

Trin grinned. "Is there a collection of dragon erotica?"

Brommin laughed. "There is, but I am not going to tell you where it is. You are too far beyond most of the males in your available age range. We don't want to make them cry."

Trin shrugged. "Their advancement is not my problem. I will never hold back to improving my mind or experience to make someone else feel like more of a man."

Sosa's expression was appalled, but Brommin was looking thoughtful. "That is a good thing to know."

Trin shrugged and set her book down on the table. "I don't have any family to embarrass, so I take care of myself first."

Sosa and Brommin glanced at each other as if contemplating life without family. Both of them suddenly looked very sad.

Trin got some fresh tea and took a seat next to the tray of sandwiches and snacks. "I am sorry that I am speaking my mind. I have been locked in dragon history for a few hours. Our ancestors thought about their environment and where they were going but not much else."

Brommin got a cup of tea for himself and another for Sosa. They sat together, and he began the quiz, "Well, in that case, how many dragon children were flown over the ocean?"

Trin nibbled at her sandwich and smiled. "Twenty-three, but four older children flew themselves."

The testing was underway.

Chapter Eight

Senator Lefarge spoke to the medical examiner via projection.

"So, Dr. Emmer, what did you find?"

The doctor cleared his throat. "She was frozen for further study and in case of identification. I examined the deceased with modern scanners, and I have come to the conclusion that she was not struck by any vehicle available at the time."

Lefarge was paying attention. "What killed her?"

Emmer pulled up a display on the screen, and the woman's face was eerily like Trin's. The claw marks broke the resemblance. The woman had been clawed across her throat, down her body, and across her belly. The dragon that had attacked her had not taken any chances. It was amazing that her baby had survived.

"Do you have any samples?"

"They are being extracted and sent to my lab. I should have more information for you in the next forty-eight hours."

"Thank you, Doctor. I look forward to any information you can provide in this matter."

The doctor took his leave, and the display cut off.

"Shit!" Lefarge shouted, and the walls hummed with the energy of his shout. He turned back to the report he had gotten from the alchemist and tried to make sense of it.

Eleven dragons were visible in Trin's bloodstream. The strongest contribution to her was a recent one. A black dragon had fathered her. There were only four black dragons, and all of them were mated and had been before Trin was even conceived. Where the hell had the dragon met her mother, and who had killed her?

He rubbed the bridge of his nose. This mystery was giving him a headache. Working on a short list of men suitable for Trin to meet was far less frustrating but a lot trickier. He had put Brommin on twice and taken him off once. There was no doubt that Trin was going to become one of the great dragons in history, but that was a lot of stress to put on his son.

He had other children, but Brommin reminded him most of himself when he was younger. If not for his wife, Orisa, he would never have gotten elected senator. Lefarge wasn't sure that Brommin would be able to burn to his brightest potential with Trin radiating power nearby.

Finding five men that she wouldn't send running on first introduction was harder than it seemed. Torm had been on the list, but now, he was off. Torm was seeking counselling and working in the sequestered part of the city until his rut wore off.

Life had gotten incrementally more complicated since Trin had appeared, but Lefarge had a sense of anticipation. There was something coming, and even his own dragon could feel the hum in the air. A catalyst had dropped in on them, and it was up to them to watch the whirlwind form.

* * * *

Trin was pacing back and forth. "The uniformity of dragoness clothing was designed to keep courting dragon males from being misdirected into an infertile relationship. Once a dragon met their true mate, they could never reproduce with someone else. As such, if a male met a good match with another shifter species, his line would never bear a dragon. Oh, and if a dragoness met and fell in love with a male who had already met their true mate, she would never have a child. That could drive a dragoness mad."

"More than I was asking for, but I will take it." Brommin smiled.

She chuckled and stretched. "Anything else?"

"Well, Sosa will test you later on the physiology of male and female dragons."

Sosa blushed. "I will try."

Trin grinned. "It is fine. I know the basics and have read the more involved details. A few hours in the erotica section and I should be able to fill in all the blanks."

"Trin! You can't!" Sosa was scandalized.

She turned to her companion. "If there is knowledge here that is open to all citizens, I am allowed to take part in it. I would rather get the average of how a mating between dragons should go by reading several different authors than taking the sterilized version out of a textbook and figuring out what the hell is going on."

Sosa blinked. "Right."

Trin chuckled. "Sorry, but I have had people telling me that I wasn't supposed to study my entire life. Every bit of knowledge I have, I fought for. It is a bit of a hot button with me."

Sosa nodded slowly.

Brommin chuckled. "I will ask the senator to give you access to the archive. You can come down here, day or night."

"After I have authorization."

He smiled. "Of course. Thank you for understanding."

"Chapter nine, paragraph three was all about obeying the chain of command because the heads of the dragon council tend to have precognition." She smiled brightly.

"So, eidetic memory will be added to the list of your accomplishments."

Trin smiled, showing teeth. "It is going to become a very long list."

Brommin gave her a look of acknowledgement, and the slight bow of his head was a nod of respect. "You will be able to take the written exam tomorrow afternoon, and then, we can make plans to have your first controlled shift."

Trin rubbed her hands together. "I can't wait, nor can she. She has been circling around behind my eyes all day."

Sosa perked up, and Brommin asked her. "Your beast speaks to you?"

"When she is very excited. Normally, it is just mumbling, but she was very chatty when I first woke up."

Brommin was pressing her. "What did she say?"

Trin chuckled. "She was looking for you. She refers to you as *the pretty one,* and all dragons are hers."

He coloured slightly. "She said that?"

"Even when you jabbed her in the hip. She could have bit you in two, but she didn't." She looked at him with a challenge she didn't quite understand in her eyes. Her dragon was controlling her attitude, and she had no choice in staring down the male dragon.

Sosa cleared her throat, and Trin winced as her body whipped around and she snarled, "What?"

"I believe that you have had enough exposure today. Please, take any books you want to read overnight, and I will take you back to your quarters." Sosa got to her feet and stood in front of her, calm but determined.

It was her friend's stoic expression that let Trin get her dragon under control. "Yes. Good idea."

She turned and went to the stack of books that she had eyeballed earlier. Trin knew that three was a likely amount to finish, so she pulled them into her arms.

Brommin glanced at the titles and nodded. "Got them. Bring them back tomorrow."

"I will, and I don't blame you if you bring the guards in. She is getting a little predatory." Trin was apologetic.

"You are coping with the activation very well. Do not worry about her impulses. As you meet more dragons, her attentions will veer to a more suitable suitor."

One of the books she had was on dragon courtship. "Thanks for understanding. Sosa, shall we be on our way?"

Sosa smiled in relief. "Yes, miss. Shall I carry your books?"

"No. I have them. Archivist Brommin, thank you for the lessons today. I have learned a lot." She bobbed a curtsey and inclined her head. Once that was done, she straightened to her normal upright posture, and she walked out of the lovely book-filled space with Sosa.

A bit of silence and some time without her dragon's favourite dragon nearby would do her good.

Before Sosa left for the evening, Trin asked a quick question. "Sosa, why are the mating regulations for dragons more strict than for other shifters?"

Sosa cocked her head. "You are just confirming what you have read?"

"I am. Why are dragons different?"

Sosa pulled her hand off the door handle. "If we want a child or any children, we need our dragons to form a match. In the lower and middle classes of dragons, this is easy. They meet and mingle, but in the higher and ruling classes, families try and manipulate the dragons into matches that are close. This leads to unions that have few, if any, children."

"So, the mention of *flights*?"

"Ah, that is a last-ditch effort to gain the cooperation of the dragons in the mating process. It plays to their deeper instincts and kicks them into a more amenable frame of mind."

"Adrenaline and the feeling of being hunted make the female choose from the males around her." Trin wanted to make sure she understood.

"Correct. It is our lot."

Trin looked at Sosa, and she saw the stress in her face. "How much longer do you have?"

"Two years. My dragon has chosen her match, but he isn't one that is in our social circle. My family doesn't let me see him."

"How did you two meet?"

"He was in an upper class when I was taking my summer course four years ago. We met and had tea in the common area, but we were not allowed to meet at any of the social gatherings. He was kept to his folk, and I was kept with mine."

Trin knew when someone needed a hug, and she got up from her desk and crossed the room. Sosa clung to her desperately, and shivers ran through her body. Silent sobs of grief that she wasn't allowed to express shook out on Trin's shoulder.

"Can you tell me his name?"

Sosa cleared her throat. "You have met him."

Trin groaned. "It was Torm."

"Yes."

"Hell. Well, that makes more sense."

Sosa leaned back. "What makes sense?"

"He wants you, but I am the mature dragon next to you, so his dragon is diverting its attentions. The answer is that I will just avoid being around him."

She nodded and swallowed. "His rut has been obvious, but I haven't been able to get near him to calm him down. Five minutes isn't enough."

"I will ask—"

"Not Sormin! He would flip."

Trin chuckled. "I wasn't going to ask your brother. If I can figure out how to do something with my two days of knowledge, I will."

"You don't have to do anything. This is just the way it is."

Trin smiled. "It is only the way it is if there is family at stake. I don't have that issue. I can be a complete ass, and the only one entitled to yell at me is the council head."

Sosa winced. "He yells loud."

"I can handle it. I am already on house arrest with around-the-clock guards. There isn't anything else they can do to me, by their own laws." She chuckled.

"I don't understand."

Trin stroked her cheek and stepped back, pulling the neckline of her nightgown down. *"At no time shall a dragon attack, consume, or destroy a marked human. All humans shall be brought to the council where their representative can argue on their behalf. All humans shall be protected and guarded by the council to preserve the potential of their blood."*

Sosa blinked. "But, you are a dragon."

Trin tapped the base of her throat. "This mark says I am human. That is the part that the law refers to. Not that I am a human but that I am marked as one."

Sosa blinked and smiled slowly. "In that case, good evening, miss. I look forward to your adventures tomorrow."

Trin inclined her head. "I look forward to providing them. Good night, Sosa."

Her companion left to go to her own room for the night, so Trin finished the last book on dragon mating behaviours. Her dragon was simmering behind her eyes when she read the dangers of mating in dragon form. Her dragon didn't see anything wrong with the idea of remaining in her winged form until the egg was laid two years after the mating.

The logistics of the aerial mating were still running through her head when she let herself sleep. Tomorrow was her test on what she had absorbed so far and if she knew as much as someone who had been born dragon. She had had more stressful grand openings.

Chapter Nine

Trin filled out and flipped over every page as quickly as she could. Brommin was monitoring a timer, and Sosa was nearby, biting her nails. Vasic was in the room and watching the test.

The stack of completed paper grew as she finished the question and answer portion and went on to the written essay. She wrote a history of dragons from the point of the crystal dragons. After reading all the books, she finally learned what made her kind of dragon special. They held invisibility in the air. Crystal dragons could fly over a village or city, day or night, and no one could see them. No technology and no living being could look skyward and see a crystal dragon. Bending light was a weird skill to have, but it meant that those with a crystal dragon on their side had a distinct advantage.

Trin finished the essay, made sure that she had completed all of the questions, and she set her pen down. "Done."

Vasic nodded and collected the paperwork. "Remain here; I will have an answer for you in a few minutes."

Brommin stiffened up. "She's here?"

Vasic gave him a grin, and he walked off with the exam.

To see Brommin nervous made Trin guess. "Your mother?"

Brommin's focus was suddenly on

her. "How did you know?"

"You look like you are a five-year-old caught grabbing a snack after their mum said no." She had experienced enough of that at the coffee shop. That was *Mom* face.

He sighed. "She has a single-minded intensity when it comes to my future."

"Ah. Matchmaking. Got it." Trin had to hold her dragon back as it bellowed an internal rejection of that idea.

"She and my father mated when he was in his early forties, so she should ease up."

Trin shrugged. "Parents always want more for their children. Well, they do if they are good parents."

He looked at her, and as she glanced over at Sosa, she saw a sad expression. She wrinkled her nose. "I learned by observation."

Sosa cleared her throat. "How did you manage to stay so friendly, being raised in federal care?"

Brommin nodded. "I have wondered that myself."

Trin pursed her lips and got up to get herself some tea. "It starts with good caregivers and teachers, and it then extends to friends and what happened to them."

Sosa blinked. "What happened?"

"Well, not every child at the Home for the Unknown is an orphan. Many are but not all. My friend Brenner lost both of his parents in a car accident, but his family was on the other side of the world. He was stuck there for six months, and he was only five years old. We made friends, and when his family returned to the area, he insisted that they take me on family events with them at holidays, and he chose to stay at the home when they had to travel on business. It was a strange arrangement, but it worked and let me see what a family should look like."

Sosa's eyes welled up.

Trin laughed. "Do you know what he and I got up to? He is a fox, and he can get into very small spaces. We explored every inch of every resort that his family stayed at. When we were twelve, we had our business plans all laid out."

Brommin smiled. "When did you meet Vasic's wife?"

"Her case was unusual. Her father had died, and her mother was being pushed into a new relationship. It was not safe for a fourteen-year-old to be around a mate in rut, so she was placed at the home until she was eighteen."

Sosa's eyes widened, and Brommin informed her, "Lionesses of childbearing age must find a new male the moment that their husband passes if they don't have an elder female to protect them."

Trin added. "The lions live by the impulse of their beast a little more closely to the surface than dragons do. Dragons have rationalized with their beasts throughout history."

She chuckled. "It doesn't always work, but while the human part is talking, the target can escape. Fortunately, dragons love a good debate."

Brommin and Sosa laughed.

"Creata is an amazing woman. She laughs as easily as she cries and gives her loyalty to those who earn it. She and I bonded over some of her university textbooks. She dropped some, and I admired the statistics text. She said I could take it to my room until I finished with it, and so I brought it back to her two days later. We were friends after that. I helped her study for her courses, and she let me share her books. When it came time for her to start going to socials, her mother hired me as her companion. I kept away the undesirables and let Vasic through the throng of men who saw Creata as a vulnerable young woman. She had a mouth like a sailor and the will of a dragon. Her mother had taught her all she needed to know to be successful in society, and she did the rest."

Sosa's eyes were wide. "I had no

idea."

"There is no reason for you to know. That is the weird point of our societies. Separating everyone into what kind of beast they are means we miss the happy moments. The laughter, the first children, the courtships, the dances. Yes, cross-blood relationships might not produce a shifter, but if enough time passes, who knows what could come of all those instincts, powers, and energies."

Brommin's eyes went wide. "Wow. You have fairly extreme politics."

She wrinkled her nose. "They are not politics, they are practicalities. Having separate social cities might be entertaining, but if folk think it is a long-term solution, they are kidding themselves. The wheel should be in every city. People need to have exposure to other types of beings, shifter or not. It broadens the mind and increases understanding."

The other two were looking at her in surprise.

Brommin cocked his head. "You agree with that, even after all the histories?"

"The histories are written by the winners. You should read what the wolves say about the dragons or the lions or the foxes. All have different opinions shaped by their own societies and customs. What the dragons saw as benevolent intervention was seen as butting in. When the dragons waited to be called in, it was seen as arrogant or ignoring allies. No one's point of view is ever all there is to see."

She sipped at her tea and paced slowly up and down the stacks of books. The others hadn't said anything since her last comment. It was a heavy topic, and it shouldn't have been brought up today. Trin couldn't help it. Her mind was filled with thousands of years of history, all pared down to make the dragons look noble, majestic, and wise.

Trin sighed. At least the dragons made a good cup of tea.

* * * *

Orisa looked at the papers, and she looked at her husband. "That is the only perfect paper I have ever seen. Even her essay is correct in every detail. Was she watched?"

Makros smiled. "She was watched. Vasic, Sosa, and Brommin were in the room with her at all times."

Orisa nodded. "So, she is a true crystal dragon. It is a good thing for her that we live in the modern era. In another age, she would have been chained in the council stronghold and only released when there was an enemy to fight."

Makros sighed. "I don't think that I would try to confine Trin. She would raze the tower and tear herself loose, only to perch on the council hall and snap birds out of the air and *then* she would transform into her dragon form."

Orisa blinked. "You would put Brommin on her list?"

"Her dragon has put him there. I don't think I had much choice." Makros leaned over his wife's shoulder and watched as she marked the page, sealed it and pressed the council seal into the ribbons.

Orisa turned her head to his and kissed him lightly. "She is good to transform. Flying will be determined from there."

"Will you do the assessment?"

"I can. I have a light schedule right now." Orisa got up and wrapped her arms around him. "Does this mean you will have time for dinner tonight?"

He chuckled. "Yes. I always have time for you."

"So says the popular senator." She wrinkled her nose. "Some days I barely see you."

"But I am always with you at night."

Orisa backed him into the desk. "You had better be. I didn't spend my early life as a hunter just to let you get away."

She pulled his head down to hers for

a kiss that reminded him who he belonged to. When she released him, she snorted a cloud of vapour.

"Oh, my dearest, I am going to be distracted for the rest of the day."

"That was my intent. I will see you for dinner." She gave him a wink and ran her hand down the front of his formal tunic before she walked away with her skirts swishing.

She left the office and paused at Vasic's desk. "She passed. Perfect paper. I am on my way down to let my son know."

Vasic got to his feet. "Please, madam, allow me."

"Oh, no. I am going to meet the woman who had the nerve to put him on her list."

Orisa Lefarge could feel the lion

shifter's frustration boiling inside him, but she continued with a determined stride to the lift that would take her down to her son's domain. She wanted to meet this woman and let her dragon take a look.

* * * *

The sound of the lift got their attention. Trin walked toward the others, and she set her teacup down on the table.

Brommin was straightening the edges of his vest and working on his posture when the doors opened.

Bronze and rubies. Trin watched the woman walk toward them, and her skin was so polished that it had a metallic look. Her hair was a rich ruby red, as was the heavy expanse of her gown.

Brommin walked to greet her, and she held out her hands. "Good day, my son. So, where is the newcomer?"

Trin fought a smirk.

Brommin turned to Trin, and he walked his mother toward her. "Lady Orisa Featherwell Lefarge, allow me to introduce you to Miss Trin Lem."

Trin made a deep curtsey but kept her gaze fixed with that of Lady Lefarge. Her dragon was rising behind her eyes, and it met the elder dragoness in a manner that Trin didn't understand.

She rose to her feet and found herself looking down at the older woman who wore her hair in an elegant twist. "It is lovely to meet you."

The lady extended her hand, and Trin reached out. The moment that their fingers connected, there was a visceral response. Trin didn't pull her hand back, but Lady Lefarge did.

"My, my. There is quite a bit of power in you, but I suppose it has been bottled up for quite some time." She flexed her fingers.

"All my life until this week. I hope to be able to give her a chance to stretch her wings. Are you here to tell me how I did?"

She inclined her head. "I am. May I have a cup of tea?"

Brommin nodded. "I will get it for you."

The lady walked around the area and took a look at the huge pile of books. She glanced back at Trin. "Your homework?"

Brommin chuckled. "Actually, Mother, she has already read them. She is ready to move on."

His mother took a seat in a froth of ruby skirts. "Good. Come and sit with me, Trin. Oh, hello, Sosa."

Sosa bobbed her head. "Good day, Lady Lefarge."

"Are you keeping track of your charge?"

"I am trying to keep up with her. It is a challenge." Sosa smiled.

Trin looked up with a smile when Brommin put a cup of tea in front of her a moment before he set one down in front of his mother. His mother noticed as well.

Trin took a seat and lifted the teacup. "Thank you, Brommin."

Lady Lefarge sipped at her tea and gave Trin a hard look. "What are your intentions toward my son?"

Trin blinked and glanced at the man in question, who was stunned, and then at his mother. "Personally, I don't know. I think he fills out his suit rather well."

Sosa choked lightly on her cup of tea.

"Mother, I don't think—"

"However, my dragon picked him out at Creata's, and she hasn't changed her mind yet. She hasn't seen his dragon, but she knows that it is hers. Is that what you mean?"

Lady Lefarge set her cup down with a firm click. "How strong is she in your head?"

"She is louder than my own thoughts when she wants to be. She can even control my body if she has to. That is not comfortable for either of us."

"Right. Finish your tea. You are going to shift. Can that dress take it?"

Trin, bemused, looked to Sosa.

"Yes, Lady. The dress can shift with her."

"Good. Instead of waiting for a matron, we will do this now."

Sosa scrambled to her feet. "Now?"

Lady Lefarge got to her feet. "Now. I will send a message and clear an area."

As if she had been there dozens of times, the lady went to the wall and pulled out the communicator. She spoke softly for a few moments and then looked at Brommin. "Bring your kit. She might get a little grabby."

He nodded and opened a cupboard, withdrawing a long flat box. "Ready."

Trin finished her tea and set the cup down. She got to her feet and shook her skirts out.

She and the lady locked eyes from

across the room, and the ruby dragon grinned. "Shall we fly?"

Trin grinned in return. "Lead the way."

Chapter Ten

The attempt to clear a transformation arena on short notice was only partially successful. The upper archways were dotted with folk who wanted to see what the excitement was.

Trin followed Lady Lefarge into the centre of the space while Brommin and Sosa kept to a safe area on the edge.

"Now, during this exercise, I will call you Trin, and you may call me Rish."

"Yes, Rish." Trin was excited.

"Right. Your first emergence was when you were having an argument. That is a dangerous situation."

"Understandable." She nodded.

"You need to be able to make the shift when you are happy, sad, or nervous. What are you now?"

"Excited, nervous."

"Good. That is a normal start. Now, I want you to pull your dragon up around you, and I want you to wear her."

"How?"

"Just get in touch with her and tell her that it is her turn."

"That simple?"

"That simple. Go ahead, Trin. I am here."

It was strangely comforting, but it was Brommin's encouraging smile from across the yard that made her close her eyes and release her beast.

She opened her eyes, and Rish was

much smaller. She was tiny. Across the exercise space, she saw Brommin, and her mind purred happily, *My pretty one.*

"Holy wings, Trin. You are huge." Rish walked around her and touched her claws and legs. "May I examine you?"

It took some concentration, but she was able to make her throat say, "Yessss."

Rish paused. "Excellent. You can speak. Did it hurt?"

Trin nodded slowly.

Rish ran her hands over the faceted skin and lifted and dropped the tail with exquisite care.

"Extend your wings, please, dear."

Trin flexed her wings and extended them then had to sidle off to one side in order to not make contact with the surrounding buildings.

"Long-range wingspan. Very nice."

Trin lifted her head and raised her wings upward, sweeping them down in a fast motion. To her surprise, she lifted up off the ground with that one swing.

"Trin! Stop that!"

She dropped back to the ground with a thud. "Sssorry."

Rish grinned and shook her head. "I do not blame you. Your body has been waiting for this for a long time."

Trin nodded.

"Well, since your physical is fine, would you like to take flight?"

Trin nodded again. Speaking was painful.

"Good. I will change and then you will follow me. Do as I do and no variations. Got it?"

Trin nodded and glanced at Brommin. Her pretty one wasn't coming along. She sighed, and the exhale flipped a spectator off their feet.

Rish stood next to her, and she chuckled. "That was fine. Now, I will be right with you. I am smaller, so there is room for both of us here. All right?"

Trin cocked her head, and Rish must have taken it as agreement. She stepped back a few metres, and then, the red of her hair and dress spread and became a glowing and translucent ruby. The dragon was small and compact. Her claws were huge, and there was a curl of smoke coming from her nostrils.

Rish nodded skyward, and she launched herself with heavy strokes of her wings.

Trin's dragon didn't hesitate. The

moment that the area was clear, she centred her body and began to fly upward.

Her dragon had to take over because Trin panicked at the height that they were achieving. Rish kept climbing, and Trin followed.

When they were so high that the wind itself was keeping them aloft, Rish began to fly across the horizon with strong flaps of her wings. Trin followed and found herself in the weird position of overtaking her tutor.

Her dragon shot past Rish, and she looked around at the sky and the land far below.

Trin was shocked at how far they had come. She felt like she could fly forever, and her beast was exhilarated by their journey, but something was nagging at

Trin's mind. She wheeled and headed back to the city.

The steady beat of her wings brought her back to the city in minutes, but she didn't want to land at the tower. She circled slowly and found her target. With careful manoeuvring, she dropped out of the sky at a measured rate. When she saw folk on the ground looking up, she tried to make herself invisible. They stopped looking, so she must have been successful.

She landed in the back garden and transformed into a human. Inside the house, there was bustle and panic. Women were running from floor to floor, and Vasic was on the com, yelling at whoever was on the other end.

Trin shook out her skirts and walked into the house. "Hello, Vasic. Baby is on the way?"

He paused and dropped the com unit. "Labour has stalled, and she refused to even try to get it moving without you."

"I am here now. Please, let the council know where I am so that no one panics." She smiled and climbed the stairs to the hall that led to the master bedroom.

She knocked on the door and then entered, seeing a sweaty and grim Creata growling at the midwife and her attendants.

"Creata, stop snarling." Trin opened her sleeves and rolled them back. She washed her hands in the en-suite, and she came back, taking up a folded towel.

"Trin. They said you couldn't come."

"I made it, Creata. I always said I

would." Trin hiked up her skirts and crawled into bed next to her friend, mopping at her brow.

Creata chuckled. "You did. I should have known you would come when I needed you."

"I will always try. I might not succeed, but I will always try."

She pulled her friend into her arms and whispered in her ear. "Are you ready to see your baby?"

"Yes."

"Then, let's get this going. I escaped my security detail." Trin held Creata's hand, and together, they started the deep breathing that would get Creata's body back in the mood.

The midwife touched Creata's belly and nodded. Trin started to tell Creata stories, and they moved her child closer to the world.

Trin was exhausted when she headed down to the sitting room where Vasic was pacing, and Brommin and Orisa were waiting.

"Lord Tal, your child has arrived. It is waiting with your tired but happy and healthy wife." She clapped him on the shoulder and sent him off.

He bounded out of the room, and Trin sat on the couch across from Brommin and Orisa. "Sosa couldn't make it?"

Orisa shook her head. "It is past her bedtime. Did you sense that the child was coming?"

"No, I sensed that Creata was in trouble. Given her condition, it was a pretty easy guess." She looked around.

"Is there any tea?"

Brommin smiled and got up, preparing her a cup of tea. "Here. Were you with her the whole time?"

"Yes. It is a good thing that the dragon thing made changes, or she would have bit right through my arm during the final push." Trin looked at her arm where the red marks had faded to pink.

Orisa blinked. "She bit you?"

"She half-shifted during her final rush to the finish."

Brommin handed her a cup, and he sat next to her. "Do you want me to take a look at the bite?"

She extended her arm. He looked at the skin and prodded at it.

"How long ago did the bite occur?"

"Half an hour, maybe more. There was blood everywhere." She chuckled.

"It didn't even freak the midwife out. She has seen it all."

Orisa leaned forward. "Did the child get blood on it?"

"No. The baby was born, and we took care of the sheets while Creata held it."

Orisa sighed. "Good. There are rumours about what exposure of blood will do to a shifter infant."

"I know."

"Really? How?"

She grinned. "I read a book."

Brommin chuckled. "That does not surprise me."

She finished the hot tea in one long draught. "Right. So I guess it is time to go back to the tower."

Orisa shrugged. "Are you hungry?"

Trin thought about it, and her stomach roared out loud in the room.

Brommin nodded. "I believe that is a yes."

Trin's shoulders slumped. "Yes."

Orisa got to her feet. "Makros is holding a table for us at the Breakith."

Trin looked at her dress, and she frowned. "I am not dressed for it."

"It will be fine. They make exceptions for us."

"Us?"

Brommin filled in the detail. "The senator's family."

"Ah. The senator's family. We tend to have long nights and run into strange substances. Our clothing is usually overlooked."

Trin nodded. "Right. Well, lead the way."

Brommin offered his arm to her and then his mother. "I brought the karros."

"Good. I could probably manage another shift, but flying in the dark isn't something that I am familiar with." She wrinkled her nose as they passed through the household where the maids were smiling, and the grandmother of the new arrival was beaming.

It was a happy and optimistic household that they left, and Trin smiled all through dinner. She smiled through the conversation about her shifting, she smiled through the questions about her future, and she smiled when the senator and his wife asked her what her intentions were toward Brommin.

Brommin merely gave her a wry glance, and he sparked her barrage of conflicting questions.

"What does Brommin want in a mate? What are his plans for his future?

What does he want?" Trin prodded at her dessert.

He blinked and gave her a wide grin. "Thank you for asking. I have always known that a woman would be chosen for me or a series if none chose me the first time. I would be put on list after list and eventually find a woman that I would like to spend my life with. I have thought about entering politics and need a wife who would understand my need to divide my attentions, but I also want a family of my own. She would need her own focus and interests. The dream woman would be one that I knew was my mate at first sight."

Trin blinked as he kept eye contact during his explanation. Her cheeks heated as he kept talking, and by the time he reached the final sentence, her skin was hot to the touch.

She gathered herself and asked him what she really wanted to know. "Do you have any personal opinion on what your mate wears?"

"As long as she is comfortable and dressed for the season, anything is fine with me." He gave her a soft grin.

She leaned her chin on her fists with her elbows on the table. "Music to my ears."

The senator was looking from one of them to the other. "So, at the winter ball, there will be an engagement."

Trin sat up. "What?"

Brommin leaned back. "Normally, your family would intercede at this point, but as you are on your own, you are at the mercy of the council."

She frowned and was about to tell

him to fuck off, but his com rang, and he got up to answer it.

Orisa smiled. "He is getting a call similar to the one that brought him to Lord Tal's house."

"That is ambitious for an archivist."

The senator sighed. "He has had training in several disciplines, but as he points out, an archivist has a lot of time on his hands. It makes it easy for him to go on the Track and Restrict missions."

Trin watched as Brommin finished his call. "Lord Minnet is trying to kill Lady Minnet. I will meet you all back at the tower."

The senator nodded wisely. "They got some upsetting news this afternoon."

Brommin bowed and left the private dining room.

Orisa gave him a dark look. "Do you know what that news is?"

He nodded. "I do. Can you take Trin on another flight tomorrow?"

"Well, I can lift off with her. She is far faster than I am." Orisa gave her a very maternally proud smile.

Trin shrugged. "My wings are bigger; it stands to reason that I would be faster."

Orisa chuckled. "You haven't read the book on dragon dynamics. It isn't actually your wings that make you fly. By the way, you are larger than most female dragons in this generation."

Trin wrinkled her nose. "It works for my human form as well, so I was not very surprised to find that out."

Senator Lefarge chuckled and got to his feet. "Ladies, I believe that there has been enough excitement for the day. My vehicle is waiting for you, so I will see you at home, love."

Orisa went to her husband and gave him a kiss that left smoke coming out of both their noses. Trin averted her stare and took in the portraits on the wall of the private room.

The senator touched a wall, and a door slid open, exposing a series of steps that he took to the roof.

Orisa sighed and walked over to Trin, linking arms with her. "Let's get you back to the tower so that you can get to that book on dragon flight styles tomorrow."

Trin walked with her, past the staff that had stayed on to prepare and serve their meal. She thanked them as they walked out and grinned at the classic karros that was waiting for them.

"Is this the senator's private car?"

Orisa gestured for Trin to get into the passenger side. "It is. I bought it for him on our twentieth anniversary. It is more my thing than his, but he refuses to part with it because of that."

Trin stuffed her dress around her legs and nodded at the doorman who shut the door. Orisa worked a rapid origami on her own skirts and slid behind the wheel. The engine roared to life, and Rish changed gears as she hit the accelerator. Trin hung on, and her flight tutor grinned, taking them through the streets at a pace that nearly approached their flight, or that is how it seemed.

By the time they got back to the tower, Trin was sure of one thing. If her hair hadn't already been white, the drive would have done the job.

Chapter Eleven

Trin focused on landing at the same spot she had taken off. The observers scattered and the medical team came in.

Rish came over and patted her nose. "Easy now. They are going to take samples to put you in our registry."

Trin focused on the older dragoness as she was measured and scraped. They tried to get a sample of her claws, but their cutters kept shattering.

"Trin, could you help them out with that?"

Trin sighed and brought her claw to her mouth. She inserted the tip and bit down sharply. There were shouts as folks scattered, but they picked up the shards with their tongs.

"Good girl. The claw will regenerate when you change again." Rish patted her on the nose again.

Trin waited and lashed her tail as one examiner got a little too personal with her backside, and the moment Rish said she could change to human, she did.

Fuming, she stalked over to the examiner who had slid his hand under her tail for his own amusement. She balled up her fist and struck the astonished medic in the jaw.

There were gasps and a few startled laughs as he was sent across the exercise yard on his back. Her back itched as she watched him get to his feet. He was angry at the embarrassment. The laughter in the space was directed at him.

Rish was watching, and she didn't intervene. Trin took her attention and put it on the man who had grown tusks and was charging at her.

The itch on her shoulders turned to a burn, and there was a tearing sound as Trin's new outfit suddenly had to accommodate wings.

Trin stepped forward, extended her hand and used her wings to propel her over the charging boar. She kicked him in the back and sent him sprawling to the ground.

She flexed her hands and her nails thickened. She straddled his back and pressed her nails to his neck. "I will bleed you dry for that insult."

He snorted and fought her for a moment before he paused. "I apologize for the insult. I did not know your skin was so sensitive."

She ratcheted his head back, and she whispered, "No lady should ever be touched without her consent. Ever. You were rude and acting like someone who didn't think they would get caught. I expect an apology from your council."

"They won't believe you."

She laughed, and it wasn't a nice laugh. "All of my comings and goings are recorded. There was a scanner on you the whole time. I think that if they don't believe the twenty witnesses, they will believe the technology. Or, you could transform, and I could transform, and we could have it out in the open arena."

He shuddered. "I will apologize and confess my error to my council."

She patted his head. "Good boy."

She dismounted, flicked her wings and walked back toward Rish. "I need another trip to Mirbella's."

Rish was covering her mouth, equal parts appalled and amused. "Why?"

"Because if I shift, I am pretty sure that this dress is going to drop. I heard something tear."

Rish laughed. "Well, we are done here. Come on, we can test your theory in your room and make an appointment with the seamstress if needed."

The older dragon escorted her back into the wheel and down hallway after hallway until they reached the lift that took her to her room.

Rish was laughing. "I have never seen so many gawkers in my life. That was hilarious."

Trin was grimly amused. "I am guessing that not a lot of ladies wear war wings into the central hall."

"They can't. They don't have them."

Trin paused outside her door. "What?"

"Women can't do the half shift. We are either on or off." Rish was still heartily amused. "You are gaining more and more appeal as a daughter-in-law."

Trin blinked. "I can do it."

"Well, I am thinking that it has to do with your lineage and that it isn't quite average for a dragon."

Trin opened her door and noted that there weren't any guards. "Where are my guards?"

"You don't need them anymore. Sosa is also reassigned unless you need a chaperone for a social event."

"Why did that happen so quickly?"

Rish followed her inside and closed the door. "You are now capable and willing to defend yourself. Even if someone attempts to make themselves a nuisance, you are able to take them down. That was our worry. It was dangerous for you to be unprotected and of breeding age. Now that your dragon has chosen for you, you are a lot less attractive to the males of mating age."

"Wonderful. Now, how do I get these wings in?" She flicked them slightly.

"Pull them in. You don't need them anymore, so let them go back to being dormant."

Trin took a deep breath, focused, and instead of pulling, she just let the wings go. The wings had taken tension to maintain, but if she dispersed the tension, they retracted.

To her astonishment, the dress didn't fall. The corset remained tight, and the wide skirt that had a nearly invisible front join was moving gently with her heartbeat.

"As I thought. The tearing sound you heard was your skin. It was like a shift only slower. It shouldn't occur again. Mirbella is an excellent seamstress. If her work can part and reform when we are dragons, a few wing extensions shouldn't be too much trouble."

Trin chuckled. "Yeah, she is a miracle worker. She understands what I need before I do."

"I must say that your taste in clothing is rather fetching. I thought it would be extreme, but it upholds the proper silhouette without being stiff or unwieldy." Rish admired the design.

"My normal clothing would be trousers and a button-down shirt with a vest. The illusion of a skirt is a concession."

"It is appreciated."

Trin went to the samovar and poured water for tea. "There is something else you wanted to tell me."

"Was there?" Rish sounded uncharacteristically nervous.

"Yes. You were going to tell me why no other woman wears the war wings."

Rish sat down at the small table with a sigh. "Ah. That. Well, it goes back to a tradition of battle between female dragons. Usually, the largest and fastest dragon would be the victor, but some of the females began to use their war form to gain mobility. The problem arises when the two females kill each other. The fighting for the best of the males became the dwindling of our civilization. Women were banned from using the wings, and after generations, they simply couldn't. There have been several moments in my own life that I wanted to fly and kick someone's ass at the same time."

Trin poured the tea. "It has its moments, but I wasn't myself. I wasn't dragon, and I wasn't human. I had parts of both, and I was missing parts of both."

She fixed Rish's cup the way she liked it and then did the same for herself. "It was disconcerting. If he had struck me in the abdomen or shoulders, I would have been toast. The only parts of me hard enough to take a hit were my wings and my claws... uh... fingers."

She sat and sipped at the brew.

"Well, as long as you recognize your weaknesses, we might be able to show you what went wrong all those centuries ago so that you can avoid the same problems."

Trin looked at her. "There is documentation?"

"Put your tea down and come with me."

Trin slammed the tea back and set the empty cup down. "You lead, and I will follow."

Rish laughed. "I have waited years to have an apprentice. Come on. We are going to visit my son."

Trin shook out her skirts, and she followed her mentor down to the archive.

Brommin met them at the lift. He seemed surprised by their arrival. "Mother, Miss Trin, is there something I can help you with?"

Orisa looked at her son. "Council business. I will be taking her to the council archive under my security clearance."

"Does Father know?"

Brommin actually backed up at the look his mother gave him. "Right. Security clearance. You know the way."

"Excellent. Thank you, Master Archivist." Orisa headed through the stacks of books, the pyramids, and containers of scrolls, and she finally paused at a structure that came to life as she wound it. A set of opera glasses elevated while Orisa turned the gears to lock them into position.

"Ocular imprinting?"

Orisa turned to Trin with her dragon eyes in place. "It is more a skill test."

She looked into the glasses and reached around them, unlatching a door that Trin couldn't see.

As the door opened, the seam in the wall became apparent. It was obviously a secret room. That much went without saying.

"Come on. The door will seal behind us."

Trin nodded and followed her mentor into the library inside the library. The door did, indeed, close behind her, but Trin didn't mind. She recognized the books, the script on the scrolls. She didn't recognize them precisely, but the hand that had written them was feminine. These were the archives of the women.

"Here we go. *Flight Dynamics* by Adolla Veil, and *A History of Queen Combat* by Venatrin Roff."

"So, I am guessing that my names come up often in dragon history?" She took the books.

"Only twice. You get reading, and I will start water for tea. For obvious reasons, you can't take the books out of the library."

Trin sighed. "I am guessing it isn't simply because there is only one copy."

"We evolve, we step back. We creep forward when no one is looking. There are other copies in private libraries and schools, but each is locked to women-only access. It is the knowledge that we need to survive that the men wouldn't understand."

Trin didn't respond. She made the most of her time and started the book on flight dynamics, committing the pages to memory before moving on. A cup of tea appeared next to her at some point, but she just kept reading. The tricks to getting more speed out of each wingbeat and an assisted takeoff were bits of knowledge she was delighted to find.

She closed the book, pushed it to one side, and opened the next. She learned the gory history of queen fights and the terrible toll it had taken on the dragons. Once, their kind had ruled the world with abandon. Mostly, benevolent rulers, they filled the skies with their armies. Then, the queen wars began. When a dragoness picked a weak mate or outlived her mate, she would go hunting for another. Having their target mated to someone else didn't matter.

The dragonesses fought to the death for the fittest mate, and one grieving, widowed, mother wanted to save her youngest daughter from that fate. She went against all shifter laws and consulted a human mage. She told him that she wanted her daughter and all daughters to come to mate with the man most suitable. Not the most handsome, powerful, or rich, just the one that would make her the happiest.

The mage agreed on one condition. Before the lock on the dragons was struck, he wanted one night with the dragoness. She traded her body for the spell.

Trin sat up blinking. "That is rather extreme."

Rish was reading another book nearby. "What?"

"That they are giving her the aura of a harlot for wanting her children safe."

"It is a common technique, and no one is as brutal to a woman like another woman. We know where to hit." Rish smiled. "Keep reading."

Trin exhaled and read on. The mage kept his word and cast the spell. No one knew about it but the widow and her daughter. As time went on, the widow realized she was pregnant, and she brought the child to term. That was when she knew that she had made an error. Instead of a soft colour, the child could bring out the strength and tone of hardened stone. She spoke to the mage again, demanding an explanation, and he looked at his daughter and laughed. The mage wasn't just a mage, he was part djinn, and the blessing that touched her daughter was a curse for the other dragons. She waited for her daughter to pick the right mate, and then, she handed over her half-breed daughter and walked to the council to tell them what she had done.

The mage disappeared, the penalty was death, and the mother met it gladly, but the curse could not be undone. The dragons were locked in the cycle of letting their beasts choose, and the population declined steeply as tradition overwhelmed need. Eventually, the new way was allowed, but the power it granted to the women was resented. Alliances could no longer be assured with the exchange of family members if the unions would be childless.

Trin exhaled as she watched the record of a whirling population grind to a halt. It had slowly started up again, but the women had to create a new role for themselves in the more restrictive society. Women were watched at all times until they were mated. It made it hard to complete your education when you were being watched non-stop.

Trin blinked. "Wait, where did the baby go? The baby should have been mentioned."

Rish laughed. "Yes, she should have been, but she disappeared from history. What do you think happened?"

Trin thought about it for a moment. "I think she went elsewhere, rejected her previous identity, found a mate and had a dozen babies."

"Based on modern genetics, it is likely that there were as many as twenty-six. We have traced twenty-six families back to that one mother ancestor."

"Holy heck, that is a lot of babies."

"Yes, it definitely is. I have five, myself. I don't regret one of them, but if I had gotten up into the double digits, I might have considered it."

"So, this is where the gem-gradient comes into the line. It is djinn magic."

"Yes and no. It is a natural evolution of our kind, but for his own purposes, the djinn sped it up." Rish smiled. "I think we will have to call it a day."

"Right. Just a moment while I finish this." She did something she had learned in school. She brought out her dragon and thumbed the pages quickly, getting a full scan of each of them.

The moment she was done, she set the book aside while storing the memory for later reading.

Rish blinked. "Does that never get noticed?"

Trin looked at her. "What?"

"Your eyes went dragon while you scanned the book."

Trin smiled and handed over the history book. "Not that they ever mentioned. I am sure someone would have told me."

Rish giggled, and Trin snickered. Together, they left the women's archive and resumed their place in the normal world.

Trin looked wistfully at the place where the door had disappeared. She hoped she could come back soon.

<h1 style="text-align:center">Chapter Twelve</h1>

Life took on a normal pattern. Brenner came in twice a week to work on the books for the shops. Trin went to see Creata and the new baby every Thursday. Trin loved Thursdays.

She was playing chess with Sosa when her chime rang. "Whoops. It is time for me to get going."

Sosa sighed. "I really wish you wouldn't walk there. I know that the council has lifted your guard, but you take unnecessary risks."

"I take the necessary risks. Since she woke up, my dragon is clawing at me for action. A short walk through the nicer parts of the city is enough to keep her paying attention during training. Why don't you ever train with me?" Trin got her cloak from the wardrobe and settled it on her shoulders. Her knives were tucked up under her corset, she had her belt around her waist, and her emergency cash was accessible.

Sosa sighed. "I can't properly fly yet."

"Oh. Whoa. Isn't that a thing?"

She grimaced. "It is. It is very much *a thing*. Sormin has tried to tutor me, as have others, but to no avail. She won't do what I ask."

Trin paused and put her hand on Sosa's shoulder. "Try letting her do what she wants to, no matter how out of control it makes you feel. You will be surprised at the results. The dragon behind your eyes is as much a part of you as the human part that thinks and speaks. She is your fire, your passion, and your freedom. Give her every bit of freedom that you have ever been denied. Think about it and give it to her. She will know what to do with it."

Sosa's eyes widened. "I don't know if I can."

"Then, you had better get used to walking." Trin didn't encourage her anymore. The words had been said. "Now, with that said, I am off to Creata's."

Sosa nodded and left the room ahead of Trin by a few steps.

Trin walked with her head high and her cloak flaring out behind her. With her white hair and startling eyes, she must have been quite the figure. She defied the tradition of dressing in her dragon's colours and instead stuck with the gemstones and shadows that she was comfortable with.

She left the dragon section of the wheel and walked outside, breathing deep of the air heavy with steam and metals. Damn, she had missed this.

The even click of her low-heeled boots was a fun counterpoint as she walked, and she enjoyed being out where the daylight could touch her again. Being in the clouds in dragon form was not the same as a walk.

The karros and other vehicles moved along, some using crystal energy, others using clean steam, and a few were manual. The key to all conveyances in a shifter city was a reduction in scent. That was why they had built air filters into all the coffee shops. The smell was fine for a while, but after five minutes, folks got jittery, so they toned it down with heavy filters in the walls and floors. Shifters were a funny lot.

She grinned and walked toward her favourite place in the world. She pushed the door open and grinned at Brenner. "Hey, buddy."

He paused and then came around the counter to give her a hug. "It is good to see you out of the wheel."

"Hey, we have been there before. Remember when we had to get zoning changed for our shops? We had to wait on the outer wheel for days before our appointment was made."

"Remember it? I have the poster hanging on the wall over there." He chuckled.

Trin walked over to the picture, and she pointed at the dragon side of the tower. "I can see my house from here."

"Did you ever wonder why they put our central government in a wheel and spoke pattern?" Brenner walked up behind her to stand next to her.

"Nope, but a quick guess would be that they are going back to ancient Rome for a lot of their traditions, including the senate."

Brenner nodded. "And karros."

"Karros is Greek. It means chariot."

"Haven't we continued our education since joining the dragons." He nudged her with his elbow.

"I knew that when I was ten. I don't know what you were doing back then."

He laughed. "I am still glad to see you out."

"They have decided I can take care of myself. I only have two bodyguards following me at a discrete distance."

He chuckled. "The two who just entered the coffee shop?"

"Yes. I am on my way to see Creata. Can I pass along a hello?"

"Of course. How long are you staying?"

"Just long enough to give her time to have a long bath so I can play with the baby."

He snorted. "I hope you are just as enthused when Niida and I have ours."

"Of course, I will be. Anyone who names me as an aunt will get the full visit and tummy-blowing treatment." She grinned. "Well, their kids will."

"You know, you are closer to me than a sister, and Niida adores you." He grabbed her hand.

She looked at the picture again. "I have been over all the dragon sections of that picture and none of the others. Isn't that odd? I think it needs to be rectified."

"Are you wanting to go to the canine section? I could totally go in and get some information about the new incentive programs for business owners."

She grinned. "I would be delighted to. Whose bright idea was it to make the building form a giant wheel on the ground, do you think?"

Brenner smirked. "Some man who lost his tire."

Trin laughed. "Well, can I get my tea? I need to give those guys a chance to finish their coffees."

She sat and had tea with her best

friend, sipping quietly when he dealt with his customers and chuckling at some of the expressions on the women in the shop.

"I think they think you are fooling around on Niida."

"No, I am pretty sure that they have read today's news report." He held up the tablet that had complimentary use marked on it.

Bastard Dragon Flies Over the City.

"Ouch. Bastard? That is a little harsh." She flicked through the images. They had been taken from the perspective of the second level of the balcony surrounding the arena. Someone was going to catch hell for that.

"The images are flattering. Your tail looks so thin in that light." He snickered. "I never would have imagined that

you would have wings. I mean I sus-
pected the tail, but that is only because I
also imagined horns and a pitchfork."

She sighed. "This is going to really
annoy the council. They are trying to
keep me out of the public eye or at least
my dragon. I think they could give a
rat's ass about me."

"Really? Flip the page."

She flicked the page, and an image of
Brommin was front and centre. *Who has
the most eligible bachelor in the city on her
list?*

There were seven women pictured,
and Trin was the last on the page. She
wrinkled her nose. "I know that it is
rude to fight over a guy, but if any of
those ladies make a move toward
Brommin, they are going to be pulling
back a stump."

"So, you have finally fallen."

She grinned. "I prefer to think of it as elevating my senses. Now that all of my friends have gotten hooked up, it is time to find a guy of my own. Well, my dragon found him. I am just agreeing with her choice."

He chuckled, and they sat for another half hour before she got up and headed to Creata's for an early dinner and a lot of baby snuggling.

Baby Amesthet Trina was resting on Trin's shoulders as she walked back and forth in the drawing room. She turned when she saw Vasic come in and blinked in surprise when Brommin, Orisa, and Makros came in. She bobbed a curtsey.

They solemnly took up seats on the

sofa, and she kept walking up and down with her sleeping niece on her shoulder. "I am guessing that this isn't a coincidence."

Orisa leaned forward. "We have a story and a request. Vasic is here because he did the research."

Vasic nodded but looked very tense for someone who had laughed with her over dinner.

Senator Lefarge leaned forward. "I know you have expressed no interest in your history, but we wanted to know, so we have found out."

She paused and then resumed her slightly bouncing walk. "What did you find out?"

"Your mother was not from the city. She was from the Delarm Valley. Her bone and tissue scans indicate that she lived there all her life. She also had genes from at least a dozen different dragons going back two hundred years. The rest of her genetic pattern was mostly human. She looked human."

He sighed. "She wasn't struck by a vehicle; she was clawed apart by a dragon while you were still with her."

Trin nodded and kept walking. If she got tense, the baby would wake, and that wasn't good for the baby.

"I know that someone left her for dead. The method just narrows the suspect pool."

Makros rubbed the back of his neck. "We know who it was. Lady Minnet. Her husband had met your mother on a business trip, and their affair resulted in you. It should not have been possible, but here you are."

"So, Lord Minnet is my father and his wife is a murderer." Trin nodded and kept pacing.

Orisa looked at her. "You are not upset?"

"I am furious, but that won't do any good." She cleared her throat. "Does anyone know my mother's name?"

Brommin added, "Leehee Anders of the Delarm Valley. It is little enough to go on."

Makros got even more serious. "Now, what do you want to do about it?"

She shrugged. "Nothing. It happened over two decades ago. My getting angry or going there won't help anything. It certainly won't help keep Amesthet asleep."

Orisa smiled sadly. "I understand."

Makros took another deep breath. "Now that that is out of the way, I have a proposition for you."

"Um, what is it?" She listened to the soft wheezing snuffle of the baby.

"My wife would like to train you as a hunter, and my son would like to train you for tactical restraint. I would like you to consider a secretarial position with the council."

Vasic was smiling slightly, and Trin looked into his features, looking for any apprehension. There wasn't any. What happened to her was going to affect his wife, so if he wasn't scared for her, she wasn't scared.

"I think I am up for all of them, but I will do the secretarial thing last, after my training." She grinned.

Brommin got to his feet and walked

over to her with a slow smile; he bent his head and feathered a kiss on her lips. When he straightened, she was holding a tablet, and he was holding the baby.

"That is your schedule. I factored in my mother's training and my own. We are doing this out of the public eye, so discretion is key. Even Sosa and Sormin can't know. Are we clear?"

She nodded. "We are clear. Just one question."

He blinked at her. "What is it?"

"Do you propose or do I? I don't like leaving this up in the air."

He leaned in and gave her another quick kiss. "I will propose at the public gathering. Just a few weeks away."

"Excellent. I look forward to training."

It was apparently the magic sequence

of words. Everyone relaxed, and the baby was handed around until she started to fuss. Vasic took his daughter in his arms and carried her up to her mother.

Trin looked at the Lefarge clan. "I am guessing that the training is for a specific purpose that I am not yet privy to?"

Orisa sipped at her cordial. "What would give you that idea?"

She looked at Brommin's serious face and the matching features in Makros, and she grinned. "This kind of acceptance comes with a price. Don't get me wrong, I am willing to pay it. I am the bastard dragon after all."

As they tried to tell her that nothing was going on, she laughed. They were lying as a unit. That was what family was all about. She looked forward to joining their weird little coalition.

Author's Note

Here ends the beginning of Trin's story. It was originally going to be all of it, but this bastard is going to be in a lot more books. Sorry.

In the next book, she learns to fight, to hide, and do what has always come naturally, pretend she isn't a dragon.

Thanks for reading,

Viola Grace

About the Author

Viola Grace (aka Zenina Masters) is a Canadian sci-fi/paranormal romance writer with ambitions to keep writing for the rest of her life. She specializes in short stories because the thrill of discovery, of all those firsts, is what keeps her writing.

An artist who enjoys a story that catches you up, whirls you around and sets you down with a smile on your face is all she endeavours to be. She prefers to leave the drama to those who are better suited to it, she always goes for the cheap laugh.

www.ingramcontent.com/pod-product-compliance
Lightning Source LLC
Chambersburg PA
CBHW061258210726
48293CB00003B/1019